Hester Hope

Roydenhurst

Vol. III

Hester Hope

Roydenhurst
Vol. III

ISBN/EAN: 9783337053505

Printed in Europe, USA, Canada, Australia, Japan

Cover: Foto ©Andreas Hilbeck / pixelio.de

More available books at **www.hansebooks.com**

ROYDENHURST:

A Novel.

BY

HESTER HOPE.

IN THREE VOLS

VOL. III.

London:

REMINGTON AND CO.,

5, ARUNDEL STREET, STRAND, W.C.

1878.

[All Rights Reserved.]

YDENHURST.

CHAPTER I.

"Now I am happy!" said the Rector, as, seated in his carriage, he drove away from Rose Cottage with the two ladies. "I am a sociable being, Miss Godfrey; I hate to be alone. I must prepare you for rather a curious specimen of domestic happiness in the pair we are going to see. My friend Sparepoint is a deep reader, and thinker, too —an excellent man. It has often been remarked that such a man, learned, shining in conversation, not only on literature, but on all subjects of interest, is lost in a retired country parish, but, upon my word, I believe the Vicar at Storkford, could never have existed there, blest as he is with a wife," and here the Rector smiled, " had he not a taste for literature. His books are his comfort, his happiness, his society, in fact."

" But has he no neighbours ? or are they not sociably inclined ? " asked Jane.

" Yes, there is no want of sociability in the neighbourhood, I should imagine ; but the truth is that Mrs. Sparepoint does not understand the machinery of hospitality ! On the wife, Miss Godfrey, devolves the—the (what shall I call it ?) the art of hospitality, how to manage those little kindnesses and attentions which are essential for keeping up the privilege of friendship and the pleasures of society."

" Oh ! then," said Laura, " I suppose we shall see a barely furnished house, and an untidy wife ? "

" No, not entirely that; but come, Miss Laura, are you inclined to **spare my** horses ?"

the Rector said, as the carriage stopped at the foot of a hill.

" Yes, I shall like to walk with you up this hill," she replied.

" Come, then," said the Rector, "jump out. See," he added, " how everything seems to be rejoicing in the spring of the year. Look at the bursting of the buds, and listen to the hum of the bee, and that mossy bank teeming with insects, each fulfilling in its order the laws of nature, teaching us how great is the beneficence of the Supreme Being, who has created and made all things living, to enjoy happiness."

" I suppose," said Laura, as she sprang into the carriage, " that it was such a day as this, with such scenery around him, that made Milton say—

> " ' To the heart inspires, vernal delight and joy
> Able to deprive all sadness but—Despair.' "

" To the pure in heart, Nature's stores are open, and from each delight and happiness is conceived, but to the unbeliever, ah—despair, indeed," said the Rector. " But here we are," he added, as the carriage crossed a bridge, and they soon stopped at a very unpretending looking green gate. They proceeded on foot to the front door, where, by the rattling of chains, and the unlocking and unbolting that sounded within, it was evident that visitors were of a rare occurrence. They were shown into a cold, dismal-looking room, where neither comfort nor elegance were attempted; the only object of attraction was the portrait of a divine, in cap and gown, and also a lady in a very primitive style of dress.

"Rather out of perspective, Laura," the Rector remarked, as she had been standing some time before the portraits.

She smiled, and said she was looking to see if she should trace a likeness in them to the worthy pair they were about to see.

The maid came to show them into another room, where, seated in an easy chair, was a venerable-looking man. He apologised for not rising, pointing to his bandaged foot.

"Sorry, Vicar, to see you with your old enemy again. How long have you been laid up?"

"A month or more. I have just managed to hobble to church Sundays. I am much obliged to you for coming to assist me to-day."

Here Mrs. Sparepoint entered the room, and when introduced to the ladies, she made a formal courtesy, and then seated herself, and Laura thought "looked extremely stiff and prim." She, however, ventured to remark it was "a fine day."

The good old Vicar perceiving she had no intention of offering any luncheon, said —

"Joan, perhaps the ladies and my friend Hartleigh may like something after their drive."

Mrs. Sparepoint got up, then dropping her hands into her pocket, produced an immense bunch of keys, and opening a cupboard, she brought out some cake and wine.

The Rector, on his return from officiating at a funeral, asked for some of the Vicar's excellent cider, adding, "there is none like this, Mrs. Sparepoint."

"No, sir, and Mr. Sparepoint may thank himself there won't be any more like that. He would go and cut down the best tree, and ever so many of them."

"They were very old, and half out of the ground; very ugly to look at," replied the old man.

"Ugly!" she repeated. "They were useful, and would have given us a hogshead or more of cider."

"Ah, well, they had their day, as well as my poor legs," he said, laying his hand on the bandaged one.

"I hope it does not give you much pain?" said Laura, who was near him.

"No, only a twinge or two now and then, my dear, to remind me that I am like the old apple trees, half in and half out of the ground. These are my chief friends," he said, pointing to a pile of books by his side. "Here I have all I want," laying his hand on a Bible. "Religion, my dear, is truly said to be a portable pleasure, such a one as a man may carry about with him without alarming either the eye, or the envy of the world." Then, thinking he was dwelling too much on the bent of his own mind, and naturally led to do so from seclusion, age and taste, he turned politely to Miss Godfrey, and remarked, "Longworth is a picturesque village, ma'am. I remember in my early days it was famous for the fishing, and very good sport I often had from the river there."

"It is still much frequented," said Mr. Hartleigh, "by strangers for the fishing."

They now took their leave of the old Vicar and his wife, and set off homewards.

"What a primitive couple," exclaimed Laura; "the old man is delightful."

"Yes," said Jane, "he reminded me of the pictures of one of the old fathers."

On arriving at their Cottage, Mrs. Tims

told them a gentleman had called. She did not mind his name, but it was the foreign gentleman.

"You knows who I means, Miss Laura. He who seed you home the other night."

"Oh, Mr. Moreton?"

"Yes, miss, I suppose that's he."

Laura smiled, and when they reached the drawing-room, said—

"What could make Tims think Mr. Moreton was a foreigner? I suppose she has mixed up Australia and the packet."

"Yes," said Jane, "she thinks every one who comes from a distance, whether in England or not, is a foreigner, for she was speaking the other day of some relation who had married a 'foreign woman,' and it turned out that she came from one of the northern counties! I am very sorry that we were out when Mr. Moreton called; perhaps he may call to-morrow."

But he did not call, and Laura looked many times that day towards the garden gate in vain. Several days passed without any tidings of him, when, as Laura was in the garden planting something from the Rectory, she heard the latch fall, and saw Mr. Moreton advancing to the door. She instantly put down her trowel, and went to meet him, just as Tims had opened the door.

"I have called, Miss Godfrey," he said, " to tell you that I hope that my Naval friend may be able to get a cadetship for your *protégé*."

" Oh, delightful ! " she exclaimed, her fine eyes sparkling with genuine joy.

" How very kind ; I am so much obliged to you, Mr. Moreton."

Here Jane came in, and Laura told her the good news, adding—

" Won't it be pleasant to be able to tell Mrs. Jasper ? "

" It will, indeed."

" Will you," said Mr. Moreton, " have the kindness to give me the boy's name and address ? "

"I am afraid," answered Jane, "that we do not know it."

"Oh, yes," said Laura, "I think we have it in a letter somewhere." And she began to look for it.

Mr. Moreton thought he had never seen any one move so gracefully. And while the sisters were turning over letters at the end of the room, that silent, grave, ladyhater, —as he fancied himself—sat there watching and wrapped in admiration.

"Here it is!" exclaimed Laura, coming forward and reading—

"'My brother, Charles Robert Jasper, he will be thirteen next December.'"

Then, finding a slip of paper, she wrote it down saying—

"I have added Mrs. Jasper's address."

"Thank you. I hope to see Captain Cravenfield in a day or so, and I shall take every opportunity of reminding him. He tells me he is pretty sure of having a cadet-ship at his disposal in about three months."

"That will be very soon," said Jane. "I suppose some school preparation will be necessary in that line."

"Yes; perhaps you will inform your friend, in order that the boy may at once be taken in hand for his examination."

"I will write to-day," said Laura, adding, "It is so very delightful to have good news to tell; I mean, news that will be a pleasant surprise."

"I am sure, Mr. Moreton," said Jane, "that Mrs. Jasper will be very grateful to you."

"No," he said, "your sister deserves all the credit. She first thought of the possibility of my having some interest in the Navy."

Then, rising to leave, he added—

"I shall very soon join my friend in Norway, and you may depend on my not allowing him to forget the cadetship."

CHAPTER II.

Now poor Mrs. Jasper was very much troubled in her mind, not knowing what to do with "that troublesome boy, Charles," as his sisters always styled him.

He was just recovering from an accident with gunpowder, he and some other boys having bought some for making experiments, and, as the frightened maid said, "nearly blew up the house; but Master Charles was always in mischief. 'Twas but the other day, Miss Lucy, he was 'most a'drowned in the pond. I do wish he could go to sea, for he'll never do no good here, and, miss, I can't put a thing down that he doesn't take it away and hide it."

"Well, Susan, I am afraid he is very troublesome, but when he gets older he'll get better."

"I fear, miss, he'll get more obstreperous."

Here the subject of their conversation was heard bawling out—

"Susan, Susan."

"What's the matter now, sir?"

"Here, come; I've cut my finger awfully bad."

"Bless me! However did you do it?"

"Oh, never mind. You women always ask 'how did you do a thing?' That's right, Lucy. You're the best of them all," he said, as she ran in with rag and thread to bind it up.

"Charles," said his sister, "I wish you would consider how you vex poor mamma by your careless, heedless ways. I am afraid you haven't a nice set of boys about you, and that they lead you into scrapes."

"No, they don't. It was I bought the powder, and proposed the whole thing; they helped, because I asked them, and they knew I'd have thumped them well if they'd been cowards. I tell you what it is, Lucy, I want to go to sea, and if mother can't send me

the right way, I must go as a common sailor,
like Crusoe. What's the use of sending me
to that stupid old Martin's; he doesn't teach
navigation—I hate Latin. What's the good
of it! I get into awful rows with old Martin,
and doesn't he wax at me!"

Here, the finger being tied up, off he ran,
and falling in with the twins, he made them
stand for him to jump over them.

A few days afterwards, as they were all at
breakfast, the letter from Laura arrived.

It would be impossible to describe the joy,
and within a few minutes, as if by telegram,
the news reached the furthest corner of the
house, where Susan was busy, and to the
garden and stable, that Master Charles had
got a piece of preferment, or at least, they
supposed his fortune was made!

How natural it was that when the first
burst of joy and surprise had passed, the poor
mother should begin to think of the reality of
parting with her son—her only boy, alas!
now—and her tears fell fast.

She thought of him launched into the world of temptation, and of the link that bound him to her being broken.

Still she knew that it must be so, and that other mothers had gone through the same trials.

There was one thing that she could always do for him, however, far away—still, she could pray for him, and the thought of this consoled her, as she busily set to work to get him prepared.

He was a high-spirited boy, with a good heart, and he told his sisters that if it was not for seeing his mother so sad, and take on so about his going, he believed he should go mad with pleasure; and as to work, he would get up as soon as it was light and set to his books, so eager was he to pass through his examination well.

The twins had peace at last, and began to wish that Charles was not always so busy.

" I do, indeed, think," said Mrs. Jasper, " that there is a special Providence over the

widow's children. How very fortunate I am
—here is a letter from Uncle Bridgnorth,
telling me that he will give Charles his outfit,
and I am to let him know when the cadetship comes."

"How very nice, mamma," said Lucy, "for
that was the only thing that troubled me.
I could not imagine how you would be able
to pay so much money, for I believe it is an
expensive business. How good of Uncle
Bridgnorth!"

Time went on, and at last the cadetship
arrived. For the few days before his going
away, the mother and son were inseparable.
He, feeling that he was going to leave her,
could not be attentive enough, anticipating
all her wishes, telling her all his little secret
hopes and fears, and making her feel more
and more that she was indeed his mother!

She was constantly to be seen going to his
boxes, putting in something with tender
thought, and ever with some belonging of
his in her hand, until he was fairly gone.

And now, how the household missed that "troublesome boy"—how quiet all was!

Lucy declared that it made her quite sad to look at that curled-up Latin grammar, over which she had so often pored with him, till it had become "one of us" with them.

With what eagerness Susan rushed in, a few days after, with "Master Charles'" first letter.

The news of its arrival brought all the family round the mother. How happy it makes them all to hear that he likes everything in his new life so much.

In the meantime what great pleasure the news of the cadetship coming so soon gave the ladies in Rose Cottage. So thoughtful, so kind of their new friend, and Laura hastened up to the Rectory, to tell Mr. Hartleigh, who had promised to write to some one who might perhaps help to get a nomination.

Finding no one at home, she sat down to the piano, and had a good practice, when at last Mrs. Hartleigh and Aunt Eleanor came in, and then Mr. John and his sisters.

" How long have you been here, Laura ? "

" About an hour.   I came to tell the Rector that young Jasper has a cadetship ! "

" What, Lucy's brother ? " said Mr. John.

" Yes."

" Bravo ! " he exclaimed, as he flung his cap up in the air, and caught it again.

" Which ? " asked his sister Fanny, " catching your cap, or young Jasper's getting the cadetship."

" Nonsense, Fan.   You know how anxious Miss Jasper was about it, and all she said."

" Oh ! then," she added, " it is Miss Jasper you are thinking of, that ' bravo ' was for her sake, was it ? "

" Just as you please to take it," and he walked off, not caring to be bantered any more.

Presently the Rector came in, and after shaking hands with Laura, threw himself into a chair, saying—

"I have had such a day of it."

"Why, where have you been, John?" asked his wife.

"To the further end of the parish. I may call it the wilds of the parish, to baptise a child, and I thought it would never be done."

"Why?" said Mrs. Hartleigh.

"Oh, the stupid mother gave me such trouble about the name. There was no one there but the old grandmother, who brought the child down; the mother was in her bed upstairs, so when I asked the name, she said 'Thos.'

"'How do you spell it, my good woman,' said I.

"'T.h.o.s.'

"'There's no such name, go up and tell the mother so.' Meantime I sat down in the chimney corner with the baby in my arms, when down comes the old woman,

"'Yes, sir, she seth there be be such a name, for she seed it herself the other day at

Bridgeton—" Thos. Hams, grocer"—and she thought as how 'twas a very purty name, and her then and there said if 'twere a by he should be Thos ! ' "

" ' Do pray go up again," I said, " and tell her that Thos. is the short of Thomas ! ' Down I sat again on the settle, but the young urchin was becoming impatient for his name, and I had to dance and dandle him; then the sheep-dog, which lay curled up in a ball, withdrew his nose from his tail, and the louder the child cried, the harder he stared at me. Between the two I was in a pleasant state; at last the old grandmother appeared, and all she said was—' Please to put it down George,' and glad I was to hand master George, roaring, over to his granny, and to take my departure."

They were all much amused, and laughed heartily.

" Well, John," said Mrs. Hartleigh, " I should have liked to have seen you dancing the baby, it is a capital story."

"Ah, I assure you I didn't half like the look of the dog when he was roused up by Master Thos."

"But what a foolish woman," said Aunt Eleanor, "the mother must be, and in these days of education, it is strange to hear of such ignorance as that."

"Foolish!" said the Rector, "not at all. Mrs. Cubbs showed immense observation and a taste for novelty too; in fact, she only carried out her own education which doubtless had been to read letter for letter, word for word. She had not come to the days of shorthand. In her time trouble was not so petted, spoilt, and worshipped as it is now, when everything is done and contrived to save a little extra work and labour."

"Come," said Mr. Hartleigh, "I must stand up for Mrs. Cubbs, for when you remember her going from the wild hill country to visit her friends in the town, I really think she showed wonderful sagacity for the benefit of her cubs, as she imagined and intended—but who is this?" he said, as a carriage drove up to the door.

"Visitors! well I shall disappear," and he left the room just before a party of ladies entered, while Laura put down the "Times" which she had been looking at, and followed the Rector out of the room. When she got home her first words were—

"Jane, there have been two mails in from Sydney lately, and I am sure by Mr. Moreton's silence on the subject, that our poor brother must have died in his debt."

"Indeed, I fear it is the case—but what shall we do? The only thing I can think of is to tell our trouble to the good Rector, and borrow of him."

"Well, I did think of that too," said Laura, "but a few days ago I heard him say he had some heavy debts to pay, and that such things always happened at the most inconvenient time."

"I am sorry to hear that. I am afraid his

nephew has been extravagant at Oxford. But what are we to do?"

"It really is very painful to feel so straitened," said Laura. "How much do we want to make up the four hundred pounds?"

"I think about £200 or £220."

"I wish I could do something to earn money," said Laura, "I could teach, but nobody would take me, I suppose."

"Why?" asked Jane.

"Oh, I have never been to the high preparatory schools for governesses, and have no names of masters for my testimonials."

"Now I have a bright idea," said Jane, "which generally comes from you in our difficulties."

"What can it be, Jane?" asked Laura, eagerly.

"What do you think my drawings would sell for each?"

"Why, they would fetch a large sum, but

it would be very dreadful to see your drawings in any one's possession."

"But, Laura, think of the necessity; for a debt of our dear brother's, and then, too, remember all that fortunate meeting with Mr. Moreton did for him. I cannot bear to feel that his debt is unpaid."

"No, of course, nor can I. It is very disagreeable to meet him, for it is the first thing one thinks of. I wonder who would buy the drawings, or where you could offer them?" then thinking a little, she burst into tears. "No, I could not bear it, your drawings shall not go. I will take courage, and tell the Rector all about it, only not till his nephew has left."

"Well, Laura, don't think any more about it just at present. Mr. Moreton will probably not come to Longworth again till the fishing season begins, and by that time we shall no doubt have settled something."

CHAPTER III.

" How gracefully that yacht is gliding round the point there! I suppose she is coming into the harbour," remarked one or two persons who were standing on the pier at Sea Cove, watching the movements of the ships dotted about. It was a lovely evening, the sun had just set, leaving a glow of brightness on the opposite cliffs, while the sky was gorgeously lined with crimson, the sea in a sleepy state. Numerous pleasure boats were to be seen in all directions. As the yacht was coming towards the harbour, a clumsily built craft was going out, which, from some carelessness, was near running foul of her, and but for the timely rush of a young lad of nineteen or twenty to the rudder, a collision must have occurred. Such presence

of mind drew the attention of an old sailor
on board, who exclaimed—

"Well done, Bob; thee has saved our
'Flora' from a nasty smash."

"That's a sharp fellow," said Captain
Cravenfield. "Is he your son?"

"No, sir; p'raps he may be if he don't go
to the Diggings."

"Does he want to go there?" asked Mr.
Moreton, who was sitting by the sailor, watching him coil up the ropes. "Does he really
want to go?"

"Aye, sir, he's 'most crazed to be off, and
'tis only my lass as keeps him away. He
don't know all the risks and chances and
dangers as I do; but 'tis my fault he wants
to go there. I could bite my tongue off for
blabbing so much about it to him."

"How long is it since you were in
Australia? Were you fortunate at the Diggings?" asked Mr. Moreton.

"I was, sir; but 'twas in the master I fell
in with was my best luck, I considered; there

isn't one in a thousand goes there such as he was."

"Who was he? What was his name?" said Mr. Moreton, becoming much interested.

"He was every bit a gentleman, sir, and as to his name, 'twas curious. I had been upwards of a year with him afore ever I heard, or thought about his name, 'twas no occasion, for 'twas all 'master' to me, and 'Jack' to he; we was never away from one another, and it was not till I heard a gentleman he falled in with up at the Mount call him Mr. Jackson, that I remember'd I never know'd his right name afore, but I've asked scores of Jacksons since, sir, if they'd a' got relations at the Diggings, and I never could find none of 'em."

Mr. Moreton was absorbed in all the man was saying. He felt convinced that this was "Jack" the sailor so often referred to in poor Culverton's Journal, and when the man went on with—

"You see, sir, I wanted to find one of 'em

to give his watch and chain to—the only valuable things I brought home."

Mr. Moreton started, exclaiming with eagerness—

" Where are they ? " Then recollecting he had given no explanation for his enthusiastic interest, said, " I know all about that gentleman, and for years I have been wishing to procure some tidings respecting him. Have you anything besides ?—any papers or documents ? "

" No, sir, only a few bits of drawings, for master was always with a pen a scribbling, and one day he did us all, and I b'lieve, sir, he sent what he wrote home by the gentleman, with, I think, a good deal of his money, to his relations. That was not long afore he joined an escort to Melbourne, to put his money in the bank."

" Have you no papers—no writings ? "

" There was nothing, sir, but some scraps and an old book or two, and I popped 'em all in an old box, and brought 'em home. But 'tis so long ago, I am feared nothing's left, except the watch and chain, which I would not let anybody have."

Here the yacht came to an anchor, and the old sailor seeing hands wanted to secure her, and knowing well his duty as master, went to the further end, while Captain Cravenfield, who had been below collecting his things, came on deck, exclaiming—

" What a splendid evening ; I am as hungry as a hunter, Moreton. I hope you have a cook in your domicile."

" Oh, yes, and if you will go on to Myrtle Cottage, and tell Mrs. Plumley to get us some dinner, I will follow as soon as I have settled a little business with the old sailor, from whom I have heard much that interests me."

He then called Jack aside, and asked where he lived, for he must see him again, and have the particulars of his late master's death, and he would go to his house. Now the fact was that Mr. Moreton hoped, by going to him, that he might get possession of the old box he had mentioned.

"Well, sir, you must go along Frog's Lane, and then turn to your right, and about half-a-mile clean out of the town, you comes right to Jack Dagman's Log—a cottage cut out of the rock. 'Tis my own, and I am proud of it, for I built most of it myself. I'll be there," but recollecting himself, "I don't know how I can. You see, sir, I takes care of the yachts belonging to the owner who lets 'em out. Howsomever, I'll be home by mid-day, to-morrow, sir."

And here they parted.

Mrs. Plumley had been bustling about with great activity, and just as Mr. Moreton reached his cottage, Captain Cravenfield was preparing to help himself, declaring he could wait no longer.

"Quite right," said his friend. "Hunger hates ceremony."

"What snug, comfortable quarters you have here; how lucky to find them. I wonder,

Moreton, you don't keep a yacht here of your own. You're so fond of sailing."

"Well, I have been thinking of it; the only drawback is that as long as my uncle lives, I should not be long away. He is getting very infirm, and last winter tried him a good deal."

"He had a seizure, had he not?"

"No, only the butler thought so, I believe. But he did not appear the least altered, and I left him as cheerful as ever, full of justice work."

"You don't allow a cigar here, I suppose, Moreton?"

"Well, I never do light one here, because of Mrs. Plumley's furniture, but I often repair to the kitchen, when she takes her departure."

"A capital plan."

And there the two friends took their cigars.

The next day Mr. Moreton set out for Jack Dagman's abode, and had no difficulty in finding it. The door was opened by a handsome young girl; he enquired if Dagman was within.

"He is not come in yet, sir, but I expect him every moment. Please to step in, sir."

Taking up the corner of her apron, she began to dust a chair, just as the door opened, and Jack appeared.

"Welcome, sir." Then looking at two or three children, he said, "Take your hats, my little dears, and go and run in the fields."

"Are those your children?"

"Well, sir, they be, and they ben't—that is, they was my wife's. She thought as I was dead, and so she got married, and so, as the father and mother be both dead, I saved 'em from the workhouse, and took 'em home, and Dorothy, she be a mother to 'em. But now, sir, you want to know about my dear master," and here the rough, weather-beaten man heaved a deep sigh.

CHAPTER IV.

"My master and I fell in with one another upon the road to the Diggings. At first all there was disappointment; still we worked on toiling for gold. After a time, sir, we got to the right stuff, and I shall never forget it; whether 'twas the bad luck before which doubled it, I don't know, but the sight of the gold 'most maddened us with joy.

"The master, he got a deal of money, and the difficulty was how to secure it; at last we proposed to join an escort going to Melbourne, for 'tis the only safe way to carry treasure, sir. The roads be full of bushmen, as ready to blow your brains out as look at you!

"When we got there, my master, he went to an hotel, and I to my sister's, where I had

my little lass, Dorothy, to school; now, sir
(he said, looking round the room in search of
her), 'most grown into a woman. Well, sir,
for a bit of a spree, I took 'em about to see
something of the country, and we enjoyed it
bravely till foul weather came, and drove us
back to our anchorage, and when I returned,
sir, my master told me he was going back to
the Diggings, and as he was so well to do, I
wondered why he should go again, and I made
so bold to say the same to him.

"'Jack,' says he to me, 'when a man is
half way towards gaining a battle, he don't
give over for a scratch or two. I have an
object at my heart which cannot be gained
without more gold, Jack, and I have made a
vow never to set foot on my native land till
I get what I want.' (Of course I never knew
what 'twas he was so earnest upon), but he
says to me, 'Now don't let me persuade you,
Jack, to come, if you're afraid, or tired of
the work.'

"I thanked him, sir, and said if he went, I

should go, too, for so long as he would be my master, I'd never get no other in any country whatsomever.

" Well, sir, we went back, not to the same place, but to quite a different part—I forgets the name of the Diggings—where we had been told there were lots of gold; but we found by the look of the holes, most as thick as a honey-comb, that lots of folks had been there, and cleaned 'em out pretty well, sir. Some gentlemen there, like master, were disappointed with the place. But there he had pitched the tent, and he thought to make a trial. However, he comed to me one day, and said he—

" ' Jack, I've made up my mind to join one or two gentlemen going far up the country. Maybe I may meet with dangers, so if I don't come back here in four months, I tell you what you must do—swap what you like, only take my books and papers to England. And here,' says he, taking down his watch and chain from a peg in the tent,

'take this, too; perhaps if I carry nothing
of any value about me, I shall escape being
murdered.' Then he looked at a locket
which he had on, and hesitated a bit. Then
he said, 'No, Jack, wherever I go, this
shall go, too, as long as I live, for 'twas
my mother's parting gift.'

"I tried to persuade him over and over
again not to go. I heard the up-country
was full of bushmen, looking out for plunder,
and that murders were constantly committed.
But he said he would 'venture,' and, says
he—

"'Jack, you are an honest fellow; if we
don't meet again, mind you take my few
things to this place,' and he wrote it down in
a pocket-book, and gave it to me, and put
some gold into it, too. But 'twas all stolen
from me before I got to Melbourne, pocket-
book and all. The worst of it was, I never
could mind where 'twas I was to take the
things, but I knowed the gentleman lived in
London, and master told me scores of times

he was to have all his money, but whether he sent it home, or what he did with it, sir, I can't tell."

"But how did you hear of his death?" asked Mr. Moreton.

"Well, sir, 'twas about two months, or not so much, after he left, a report spread of a party being attacked, and some of them murdered; but I didn't think 'twas my master, so I stopped on for near six months, and then I began to fear 'twas true, and I determined to go to a place on the way up the country, and try and find out more particulars, and there they told me of a store further up, where I should perhaps hear more. From all I gathered about the party who had been missed, I felt sure it was my master, and as I was thinking what to do, the man at the store said, ' here are some things brought to me, which were picked up near the place.' I didn't know any of 'em till I came upon this here locket, and then I knowed all at once the truth. I paid for it, and left for Melbourne, and there, sir, I had a chance of a voyage which took me over six months, and then I brought my little lass over here, and bought this bit of roadside and my log-house, and thanks to my good master for it. He made me save up my money—"

"You mentioned his watch and chain?"

"To be sure," he said starting up, "I did sir;" he went to fetch it, and soon returned, handing to Mr. Moreton a discoloured watch, with chain, seals and a locket. Whilst Mr. Moreton was examining them, the old sailor went to a side door, and called, "Dorothy," asking her what had become of an old box, which used to be on the top of his bed."

"Isn't it there now, father?"

"No, child, go and look for it."

She went to the door, hesitated, and then came back saying—

"Father, I gave the box to the children."

"Smash my timbers," said the sailor, "but where are all the bits of papers, and old books that were in it?"

" I don't know," she said, " gone I'm
afraid, 'tis such a long time ago, father."
She left the room and soon came down with a
few pieces of paper, and a half-drawn map.

" This is all I can find, and there are some
old books on the top shelf, which I can't
reach." The father went up with her, and
they brought down an old Bible, one or two
books on geology, one on Australia, and a
roll of maps, with a few unfinished sketches.
Mr. Moreton saw them all packed up for
sending to his cottage, then he said—

" Is there anything that I can do for you ?
Your faithful conduct to my friend, and your
honest heart shall be rewarded if there is
anything within my power to do for you."

The old man was quite overcome, he thanked
him, saying—

" I have employment, sir, at present, but
what I should like, would be to be master to
a gentleman's yacht, as I only act under the
owner of two yachts here, who lets 'em out,
but he is not a gentleman, sir."

" Well," said Mr. Moreton, " I am thinking of purchasing a yacht for myself. Should I meet with a good one, and when I do, you shall be master."

Here Dorothy pulled her father's sleeve, whispering—

" Put in a word for Bob."

" Thank you, sir; nothing I could desire better than to be master to your yacht, and 'make so bold, but if you should want to have a good lad, the youngster on board the ' Flora' yesterday, who was so sharp in saving her from an ugly blow, would be a first-rate sailor, sir."

" Certainly, I'll not forget him," and he noticed the blush and pleased look of the girl as he assented.

When Mr. Moreton returned home, he found that Cravenfield had gone for a long walk, so he sat down to examine all poor Culverton's papers minutely. They were, however, only scraps, chiefly calculations. On one or two, the word Roydenhurst appeared, on another, as if for a memorandum, the name torn off, " lawyer at Melbourne," a pencil sketch of the Diggings, the figures in which were evidently those of himself, and Jack, and the dog Dratt, for " Dratt " was written under it. This was all that Mr. Moreton discovered. He then looked over the books ; in one was written " bought at Melbourne," in another, " bought of a lucky Digger." The Bible was old and worn, inside it was written, "Richard, from his mother," it was covered with coarse canvas, which smelt so strongly of mildew, that Mr. Moreton took out his knife, and cut the covering off, when his knife ran into a piece of paper within. He was not a second in taking the cover off, and there lay a piece of paper folded, the exact size of the book ; he eagerly opened it, and read at the top, " My will," then below, " The will of Sir Richard Culverton, Bart." For a moment he hesitated whether to open it, but thinking he might be of use to the sisters, he read on—

" I, Sir Richard Culverton, Bart., of the County of Cheshire, in order to bequeath the money which I have now deposited in the Government Colonial Bank, in the following manner, make this my last will and testament, if I am not heard of in five years from this date.

" In the first place, I desire that my debt of four hundred pounds, be paid for Philip Moreton, Esq., into the hands of his lawyers, Penhorn and Co., Bryant's Court, London. To my sisters, Jane Culverton and Laura Elizabeth Culverton, I will and bequeath the sum of two thousand five hundred pounds each.

" To my valued friend, the aforesaid Philip Moreton, I will and bequeath one thousand pounds, as a small token of my gratitude to him.

" To Mrs. Rebecca Jasper, the mother of the late Herbert Jasper, I will and bequeath the sum of five hundred pounds, or if the said Rebecca Jasper be not living, to her children. I will and bequeath to my old nurse, Mrs. Mary Tims, the sum of one hundred pounds.

" Should either of my sisters not be living, the whole is to go to the survivor, or should neither of them be living, the whole five thousand pounds is to revert to my friend, the said Philip Moreton, whom I appoint executor of this my Will."

Here it was duly signed, sealed, witnessed, and dated, " October 10th, 18—, Melbourne." Mr. Moreton folded it up when he had read it, and was going to put it back, but the cover was so mildewed, that he thought he would rub it off, and in drawing off the other side, he observed some pieces of paper stuck at the back of the book.

One of these was a banker's draft for £200, " for immediate use " written upon the paper over it; others were receipts from bankers, with whom he had deposited his money.

Mr. Moreton sat so deeply absorbed in thought, that he heeded not the entrance of

his friend, nor until Captain Cravenfield exclaimed, " Why, Moreton, what has thrown
you into such a brown study?" was he aroused.
" What have you here?" and the Captain
took up the old canvas cover, and then the
discoloured watch.

" Why, a most extraordinary circumstance
has come to light, and all through a mere
trivial accident."

" Well, Moreton, it is the spark, you know,
that produces a raging fire—a single word
decides the fate of thrones, dominions, prince-
doms, powers."

" True enough," replied Moreton, " small
occurrences ofttimes bring forth great events,"
and then he related some part of his old
friend's history, and concluded it with, " I
must go to the village of Longworth about
this business, for his relations reside there."

" Longworth, near Shoptown?" asked the
Captain.

" Yes."

" Oh, I used to know that place well, it

was a capital spot for fishing. I was then a chap at the Grammar School, at Shoptown, and often we boys rambled over to Longworth to fish. I remember a famous inn there, where we got our fish cooked, and had many a good dinner on spree occasions. I wonder who the Rector is now, there was a queer old man there in my day, a regular huntsman."

" Mr. Hartleigh is the present Rector."

" Indeed! is he related to John Roach Hartleigh, I wonder."

" He had a nephew, an Oxonian, staying with him the other day."

" Ah, the same. I met him at an old friend's. I should like of all things to see my old haunts again. I'll go with you tomorrow."

" Do," he replied, " and you can ride my groom's horse."

" Very well, so I will; that's a capital plan."

But it was not to be, for Captain Cravenfield had a letter the next morning, summoning him home at once, as his sister's wedding was to take place immediately.

" Well, but you can come afterwards," said Moreton. " They won't want you at home when it is all over."

" Will you remain there, Moreton ? "

" Yes, I shall stay there till this business is settled."

" Then I'll run down, and take a peep at my old haunts again. There's something very pleasant in going over places you remember only when a boy. Old thoughts, old pleasures, old faces come before us, connected with the days of our youth—happy time, never forgotten, never to be again."

CHAPTER V.

PHILIP MORETON was on his way to the little Cottage at Longworth, when he met Laura going into the village.

Her genuine expressions of surprise, tinged with a tone of pleasure at seeing him, gave him quite a new sensation—he had never before received so sweet a smile of welcome.

He asked if her sister was at home. She replied in the affirmative, and proceeded on her way to the village.

Philip Moreton, instead of going on to the Cottage, returned to the inn, where he waited until he thought both sisters would be at home.

Why was he so anxious that Laura should hear from himself the news which he had to communicate? Because he liked to watch her beautiful expressive eyes; he knew not why, but her gratitude to him for young Jasper's cadetship had given him an indescribable pleasure.

On Laura's return, her first exclamation was—

" So, Jane, you have had a visitor ! "

" No ; I have seen no one. Who have you met ? "

" Mr. Moreton ! and I really thought he was coming here."

" I dare say he will call to-morrow," said Jane.

" It is very strange. I felt sure he was coming here to see you ; but here he is," she added, looking out of the window.

Miss. Godfrey rose to welcome him, expressing a hope that he had escaped all sorts of dangers from the falls and precipices of the Norwegian dangers ; to which he replied he had, and that he wished often, while surrounded by such scenery, that he had been an artist.

Then he told the sisters of the extraordinary circumstance which led to the discovery of the sailor " Jack," and, he added,
" your brother's will."

" Oh, Mr. Moreton ! " they both exclaimed,
" is it possible ! Where is the sailor ? How
can we see him ? "

" We will see about that, Miss Godfrey ;
but, in the meantime, I have brought you
this "—taking a parcel out of his pocket—
" It is his will, with his watch, and a few
scraps of paper."

" His will ! How extraordinary, after so
many years, it should now come to light, and
that by a mere chance ! "

" Yes, indeed," he said, " it is wonderful
how events, little expected, come to pass, and
how a man's nature may change by circumstances."

Then, as if he had caught himself uttering
his thoughts, he abruptly took leave, saying—

"You will see, after reading this paper, that it will be necessary for me to see you again, Miss Godfrey."

The frequent consideration of a thing wears off its strangeness, and shows it in many different lights.

The sisters had long dwelt on their brother's history, and of his death, and their well-regulated minds had taught them a patient submission to the will of Providence.

They sat in silence for some time over their treasure—relics of their dear brother. It was painful to them to look at these things; but there was much to comfort them. His will gave fresh proofs of that good heart which in boyhood had, in many little acts, so delighted their mother. He had not forgotten his old nurse, and his bequest to Mrs. Jasper told of the respect he felt for her son. And what an immense relief it was to them to find that their brother had not only mentioned his debt, and refunded the money, but had, from a sense of gratitude to Mr. Moreton, entrusted to his care the management of everything.

" We will not yet write to tell Mrs. Jasper of this money, in case there should be any disappointment about it."

" But, Jane," replied Laura, " what can go wrong ? What disappointment can there be? Mr. Moreton will see to it all ! "

" Yes ; I am sure he will; but you know the money may not be so readily given up ; at all events, you may be sure there will be some delay, and probably trouble, to get it."

Miss Godfrey was right. Difficulties did occur; and time passed on without any hope of the money ; for although Mr. Moreton had sent, through his lawyers, the needful certificates, signatures and information required, yet the flourishing firm in Melbourne were taken by surprise. For as year after year passed by, they clung closer to the unclaimed property in their possession, and now were not disposed to relinquish it too easily at the request of an Executor who, they would fain believe, had suddenly pounced upon some obscure document, and made it an instrument for wrenching the money from their hands. " Possession " they held to be " nine-tenths of the law."

There are men enough in the world capable of getting up plausible arguments, who promise themselves security in any designing action.

Mr. Moreton was resolute of temper. He would suffer no man to cringe or fawn to him—nor would he accommodate himself to any man's humours. Sincere, without guile, he was not ashamed of being true to all the sacred offices of friendship.

The Bankers' incredulity, the Lawyer's offers, their arguments, the attempt to set aside his friend's will, all made him indignant. And in this frame of mind, he hastened to the Cottage one day to communicate the cause of delay to the ladies.

"I am extremely sorry, Mr. Moreton," said Miss Godfrey, "that you should have so much trouble with such disagreeable people—and, indeed, I was afraid that there would be great difficulties—I mean, they might dispute the will."

"Disgraceful—they dare not! I will not spare them from the law—the conniving rascals!"

Then, as if he thought his feelings had made him for the moment forget his being in the presence of ladies, he said—

"Pardon me, Miss Godfrey, injustice and deceit rouse my indignation. When truth is clear before me, I can ill brook such letters as those; but the impartial jurisdiction of the law will help us."

She replied—

"I am afraid that law will be a very great expense, and, should we fail, we are not prepared for that call."

"Forgive me! As Executor, it is my pri-

vilege and duty to see my friend's will duly
honoured. Of the law part you will know
nothing."

Then taking up his hat, without waiting
to be thanked, he added—

" Excuse my abrupt departure. I wish to
be in time for to-day's post."

After he had gone, Laura said—

" How very good he is ! But did not his
voice and tone of indignation remind you of
that night at Myrtle Cottage, when, as he
passed our door, he was so angry with Mrs.
Plumley ? "

" No ; I did not observe it. I was too
much absorbed in thinking how to let him
know that we could not afford to pay law ex-
penses in case of failure. He is, indeed, very
kind, and from first to last has been a true
friend to poor Richard."

Time passed on. Mr. Moreton called
often, and had to go backwards and forwards
to London, till matters were at last fairly

settled respecting the will, and in due time the money was paid.

When Mrs. Tims was informed of her legacy, she could scarcely credit the fact—the great distance seemed very much to enhance the value.

" That Master Richard should, so far off over the waters, think upon me, 'tis that, Miss Laura, that surprises me—and growed up to manhood, too—'tis few gentlemen troubles themselves about their old nurse ; there "— and she applied the corner of her apron to her eye—" Master Richard was always so affectionate— such a merry, handsome boy—he used to play his old nurse fine tricks."

" And I dare say for my dear mother's sake, Tims, you became attached to him and my sister."

" Yes indeed, Miss—sweet lady ! " she sighed out. " But to think of a hundred pounds falling to me ! Dear me, whatever shall I do with it, Miss Laura ? "

"You will, no doubt, Tims, find many things to do with it. There are your brother and sister to help."

"They don't want no help, miss, though, of course, I mean to give them a bit of it. But, you see, if they was to have a deal of money come unawares upon 'em, it would, maybe, unsettle 'em. Please, Miss Laura, don't be angry with old Tims, but if Miss Jane and you would take half of it, I should be so pleased, so happy."

"Oh, no, dear Tims," said Laura, "not for any consideration. So pray put such a thought out of your head, though, indeed, it is just like your generous, unselfish heart to have suggested it. We will keep it safely for you, and let you have any or all whenever you like."

But the hundred pounds caused Mrs. Tims much thought and trouble, and many nights, she said, passed in thinking upon it, until, one day, some extraordinary and bright idea took hold of her mind, and made her watch for Mr. Moreton's leaving the Cottage in the evening, to go out at the back door to catch him at the little gate. It was dark, and the shutters were closed, so that no one saw her waylay him, and stand talking to him in the road, as follows—

" If you please, sir, if I don't make too bold, may I speak to you ? "

" Certainly, Mrs. Tims, what is it ? "

" Why, you see, sir, Master Richard's hundred pounds."

" Yes, I know ; I hope you have it."

" Oh, dear, yes sir, but 'tis how to dispose of part of it, sir. I thought p'raps as how you might be able, if 'tis not taking too great a liberty, to help me to buy a pianer."

He gave a little start.

" For yourself ? "

" Dear me, no, sir. You know what I mean, sir."

" No, Mrs. Tims, I don't."

" Well, then, sir, it's for Miss Laura. They've a got none; and I've often 'most cried to think how different things is here as they should be, or, at least, as they was in my lady's time at Roydenhurst. And now I've made up my mind that some of this £100 shall get Miss Laura a pianer, for she have got such a bootiful voice."

"Well, Mrs. Tims, how much of the money do you wish to give for the piano?"

"Well, I thought of sixty pounds, and divide the remainder between my brother and sister, sir. You see, it don't do for poor folks to have too much money, it makes 'em feel discontented when it's all gone."

"Well, I'll think over this business. It will take some time to find a good instrument to suit Miss Laura Godfrey."

"No doubt, sir. But will you please not to say a word of it to them in there (pointing to the window) till 'tis done."

"Very well, Mrs. Tims, I'll keep your secret, you may depend," and he walked away, extremely diverted at the scene altogether, and admiring the old lady's devotion and pride in her ladies, and all relating to them.

Some few days afterwards, Laura met her with a quantity of old music books, which she had been hunting out of boxes in the lumber-room, and was now busy dusting them.

"Why, Tims," said she, "what have you got there? music books!"

"Never mind, Miss Laura," she said, with a complacent, self-satisfied air. "Music don't sound shut up in a box; 'tis time 'twas out, I'm thinking."

"What can Tims mean?" said Laura, "I heard her upstairs rummaging over the boxes, and soon afterwards I met her on the stairs with a heap of music books."

"Oh, some of her odd, quaint ways of reviving old times. She told me one day that, whenever she felt sad and out of spirits, she liked to turn over old times in her mind, and take a look at the pictures of Roydenhurst."

CHAPTER VI.

WHAT was it that kept Philip Moreton so long at the quiet village inn? and why was he unable to fix what day he should leave it? Even his groom wondered at his master's unusual want of decision and energy. Captain Cravenfield had long ago written word that he could not come down, so he could not be waiting for him.

"Here," said Mrs. Hartleigh, reading a letter one morning at breakfast, "here is a request, John, from the Ladies' Committee at Shoptown, asking me to be a patroness to the ball, which is to take place on the 24th, for the benefit of the hospital. What shall I say?"

"Say!" repeated the Rector, "why, that you will take as many young people as you can. Let me see, there are Fanny, and John, and Laura—take her, won't you?"

"Yes, it will be her first ball. I shall give her a dress for the occasion, and undertake it altogether; and I shall give Fanny her choice—of a new dress or the money. But, as she has had a new one lately, I dare say she will prefer the latter."

"Will Mr. Moreton go, do you think?" said the Rector.

"Perhaps he may; you better ask him."

"Very well, then; say you'll take half-a-dozen tickets, and with regard to the girls' dresses, settle it as you like, my dear Mary, only don't let there be any jealousy. But I hope Fanny is too sensible ever to fancy that our partiality for Laura could affect our love for her."

"Very true; besides, she is so fond of Laura, and admires her so much."

The young people were all delighted, and for some days nothing was talked of but the coming event—of a county ball.

"I wish, Fan," said Mr. John Hartleigh, "that the Godfreys would ask Lucy Jasper to come for the ball. Can't you put it into their heads?"

"Oh, John, think of the distance and the expense. I am sure they would think it quite foolish."

"Why, nonsense! the journey would not cost much. You are always thinking of the expense; everything is an expense to you."

"Well, I suppose people who are not well off ought to count the cost before they do anything that is merely for pleasure, and not for necessity?"

"Are the Jaspers so very poor, then?" asked he.

"Yes, very, I believe."

Here there was a long pause. At last he said—

"What can a fellow live upon?"

"Live upon! what do you mean? That depends upon so many things."

"Suppose, then, I mean—marry upon?"

"Oh," said she, "that must be according to the style you live in, and the establishment you mean to keep. But I hope you are not thinking of anything of the sort yet, John?"

"No, not yet, of course," said he, "but it's a confounded bore to be without tin," drawing his fancy pipe from his pocket.

"I am afraid, John," and she spoke playfully, "that these little fancy pipes won't agree with the study of, 'what can we live upon.' They will overbalance the necessaries of life."

"Nonsense! such trifles as this—"

Here the entrance of his uncle interrupted him.

"John, as Mr. Moreton says he never goes to balls, we must find another gentleman. Do write to Felix Moore, and ask him to come for the ball."

"I don't think he's at home, uncle, but I will write to him directly."

And he went off to do so.

The anticipation of the ball gave great delight to all the young people, and when Mrs.

Tims heard of it she was extremely pleased, thinking, perhaps, less of the pleasure for her dear Miss Laura, and more of the secret pride she felt that "they up at the Rectory," should at last see "our young lady" dressed as she ought to be. This had long been her wish, ever since she saw the gaily-dressed party go off to the dance without her; and now, here was a most unexpected opportunity of showing her favourite off to advantage, as she considered it.

There was, however, something that made that worthy old servant anxious as the time drew on. It was not the dress part of the business—she knew that would be all perfect, since the Rector's lady had undertaken it— but there was something on her mind, and at last, finding herself alone one day with Miss Godfrey, she determined to speak to her.

"Miss Jane," she said, somewhat anxiously, "Miss Laura haven't had the advantages like other young ladies. You knows what I means, Miss Jane—about this ball. I don't mean to say she don't dance well, but p'raps Miss Laura don't know the new ways, and I was thinking, Miss Jane, if she was to see Mr. Pointerlow, he that teaches to the ladies' schools, he might put her in the way, like. There's no one who will look so well—nor behave better—but I should be so vexed if Miss Laura, when she comed to be at the ball, didn't know the right's and left's. You knows what I means, Miss Jane."

"Oh, yes, Tims," said Miss Godfrey, laughing. "I know that you are so devoted to my sister you wish her to be thought perfect in everything; but I am sure you need not be afraid of Miss Laura's feeling herself at any loss in the dancing part, for she has been so much with the young people at the Rectory that she has, no doubt, learned the 'new ways.'"

"Well, so she have, Miss Jane, and I have no doubt she will outdo 'em all—in appearance, I know she will. You may depend upon it, Mrs. Hartleigh will be proud enough of her that evening."

Here the object of the worthy domestic's solicitude and anxiety appeared at the window, laden with flowers.

" See! dear Jane, what a collection! I had gifts offered me at each cottage, and though I would much rather not have had them gathered, I was afraid to wound some tender attention if I refused."

" I am very fond of some of the old-fashioned flowers, only to be met with in cottage gardens now," said her sister. " But, Laura, Tims has been lamenting your having forgotten your dancing lessons, and proposes sending for Monsieur Pointerlow, before the ball."

" No! really—has she ?" and Laura was very much amused.

At that moment Tims brought in a flower glass, saying—

"I brought this for your flowers, Miss Laura."

"Thank you. Are they not pretty?"

"Yes, miss. This is what my sister is so partial to. We calls it 'Wonderful Widow.'"

"I think it is a 'Scabius,'" said Laura. "Is your sister any better since her illness?"

"Yes, miss, a deal better since she took that medicine Miss Jane took when she was so ill."

"Do you mean tincture of bark, or columbia?"

"No, miss; I think 'tis what you calls 'Queen Ann.'" *

"Oh, quinine!" exclaimed Laura, smiling.

"Why, yes, miss; 'twas like that."

She went off, quite satisfied that she had made herself understood.

"Tims would have been a capital linguist," said Laura. "She takes so quickly to sounds, and dashes off a word to suit the sound as well as the meaning."

* A fact.

"Yes; and she is not at all shy of speaking it out, because she has her 'you knows what I means,' at the end."

As Miss Godfrey had again expressed a great wish to see the old sailor "Jack," if he could be persuaded to come to Longworth, Mr. Moreton determined to go over to Sea Cove and propose it to him.

On knocking at the door of the log house, a voice within said, "come in."

No sooner did the young woman see who her visitor was, than she came from the fire, on which was something she was cooking, and begged pardon for not going to the door.

"But I thought, sir, 'twas pr'aps the doctor —father's very bad, sir."

"Indeed! I am sorry to hear it. What is the matter with him?"

"Well, sir, I don't know; 'tis his head, sometimes he rambles like. Please walk upstairs, sir, and see him."

It was not very easy to mount those very crooked stairs; but Mr. Moreton did reach the room above, where lay the old sailor, who did not know him, and took him for the doctor. As he saw he could do nothing to relieve him, he descended to the kitchen.

"Are you alone with him?" enquired Mr. Moreton.

"Yes, sir; that is, Jim and me."

Then, looking somewhat shy, she added—

"I think father took a chill the day we was married. He took us for a sail, sir, and the weather was 'most too cold; but father, he would go, and Jim and me didn't like to thwart him."

"Let your father have whatever the doctor says he requires," and he put some money into her hand.

"Can you write?"

"Yes, sir."

"Then let me know how he is. There is my direction," and he gave her a card, and left the man's hut, to return to Myrtle Cottage, where he had not been more than a couple of days when he received the intelligence of the old sailor's death, which did not surprise him, after seeing how ill he was.

He could not, however, help thinking of the disappointment this event would be to the sisters, who had frequently expressed a wish to see the companion and servant of their brother.

Mr. Moreton told the landlady of the Three Oaks that he was going away; but as he would return at the end of a week, he desired her not to let his rooms.

It happened that Captain Cravenfield, having finished the business that detained him at home, thought he would take his friend by surprise, and arrived at Longworth in his absence; and when Mr. Moreton rode up to the inn on his return, a well-known voice greeted him from the window.

"Better late than never. Here I am, Moreton—come at last—taken possession of your room."

"Glad to see you, Cravenfield," said his friend, as he entered. "When did you come?"

" Wednesday evening—and I have already found old friends here ; first in the Three Oaks, on yonder board. They haven't grown a day older. And the village shop, where I used to invest some shillings, is just the same ; but the Rectory is new, and what a nice place it is ! "

" Have you been there ? "

" Yes ; I dined there yesterday, for Mr. John Hartleigh happened to hear of my arrival, and the Rector kindly called and invited me to dinner—and by-the-by, Moreton, there was a remarkably pretty, elegant looking girl there. Is she a niece ? "

" A niece is staying there, but I don't think she is remarkable for beauty."

" Oh, there were two young ladies, one, as you say, nothing uncommon. They want me to go to the ball on the 24th, but I am afraid I shall not be able to stay for it. Are you going ? "

" No ; I don't care for balls."

A day or two after, when Captain Cravenfield came back from calling at the Rectory, he exclaimed—

"I have seen that graceful girl again. I wonder whether she is a relation. I had the pleasure of escorting her down the hill to a cottage. I only heard them call her 'Laura.'"

"No," said Mr. Moreton. "She is not a relation; she is one of the ladies at the Cottage."

"Well," said his friend, "she's worth looking at."

Mr. Moreton said nothing, but thought his friend had good taste, and he knew he was a judge of beauty. There was a pause, interrupted by Captain Cravenfield saying—

"I think, after all, I will go to this ball. I may meet some of my old schoolfellows there; it will be rather pleasant to see what changes time has made in the old town."

Here a note was brought in to Mr. Moreton; he read it, and said—

"An invitation to dine at the Rectory to-morrow. What say you?"

"Go, by all means. It may give me a chance of seeing my beauty again."

Mr. Moreton rose to write his answer, and his friend did not see the expression of displeasure in his countenance at the words " my beauty."

They were all at the Rectory much pleased with the Captain's gay and cheerful conversation.

He was again lucky in falling in with the Miss Godfreys as he was coming back from the Rectory one morning, and stopping to speak to Laura, she introduced him to her sister. They liked to hear his reminiscences of old times there, and asked him one or two questions as to what the Cottage was in the old Rector's time, and were amused at his description of those primitive days, which had made a strong impression on his youthful mind.

He returned to the inn in high glee, and spoke of his good fortune in meeting again the prettiest girl he had ever seen in his life, and her very interesting looking sister, whereat Mr. Moreton shoved his legs about, stabbed the fire, and lighted a cigar.

The day of the ball arrived. It had been arranged that the Miss Godfreys should spend the afternoon at the Rectory, where the gentlemen at the inn had been invited to dine. Although Mr. Moreton was not going to the ball, he could not resist the pleasure which he was conscious he felt in the sisters' society.

"Oh! how beautiful," exclaimed Laura, as she entered her room, where, laid out on the bed, was a white silk ball dress. "Dear Mrs. Hartleigh," going up to her and kissing her, "how very, very good you are. I am afraid this is a most expensive dress."

"Not at all too good, my dear," she said, playfully, patting her cheek, "for the wearer; now take your time, there is not the least hurry, we shall not leave this until after eight o'clock."

"Look, Jane," as her sister entered. "Is

not this lovely?" holding a spray of water lilies in her hand.

"It is, indeed, all in exquisite taste. Now let me do your hair."

"I wish, Jane, that you were going too."

"I shall enjoy the account of it all from you," then looking at her youthful sister with quite a mother's pride, "you look extremely nice."

"She do look bootiful," said Mrs. Tims, holding up a candle as high as she could. "And dear me, Miss Jane, don't she look just like the pictur of my lady over the fire-place at Roydenhurst?"

"Yes, she does," she was then fastening a beautiful pearl necklace round her sister's neck, "this is the same necklace, and now, dear Laura, it is yours."

"Oh, dear Jane," throwing her arms round her sister, quite regardless of what injury she might do to her dress. "Thank you so much."

"Take care! take care, Miss Laura," said

Tims, "You will squash those bunches of lilies to the side of your dress."

"Never mind, Tims, they'll be all right again," shaking them out. "Now I suppose Mrs. Hartleigh will expect me to go to her room. I should rather show myself to her alone, than be inspected below."

But here that good lady came in, herself in full dress, and settled the matter.

"I am come to have a look at you, my dear, in private. Oh, extremely nice! I am more than satisfied. I feel quite proud of my young charge. Fanny, too, looks very well. She is gone down; are you quite ready?"

"Yes," said Jane, "the finishing touch has been given."

When they entered the drawing-room, Captain Cravenfield became quite excited, he would not have missed this ball on any account. He was eager to claim Laura for the first dance; she said—

"Thank you, but I long ago promised to dance with Mr. John Hartleigh."

" Well then, will you the second and fourth,
Miss Godfrey ? "

To which she quietly said—

" Yes."

How Mr. Moreton envied his friend, while
he silently looked on, lost in admiration.

After the happy party had all driven off,
Philip Moreton returned to his inn. As he
sat alone in his silent room, he could not get
the sound out of his ears of that sweet voice,
and the quiet " yes."

"How I envy that fellow Cravenfield,"
thought he, " he has such a way of getting on
with people, so free and affable. I wonder
how he dances," then he got a book and tried
to read, but it was no use. He again and
again found himself thinking of that graceful
form, and the wish to see her again grew
stronger, until at last he started up and rang
the bell. " John, get my things out, I am
going to the ball ; have the dog cart at the
door in half an hour."

" How master is changed to be sure ! why

I have lived over ten years with him, and I never knowed him go to a ball afore!" said John to himself as he laid out evening clothes for his master's toilette.

The ball-room had become so crowded by the time Philip Moreton arrived, that he was obliged to remain for some time close to the door. It was a gay and lively scene, but he cared not to seek amusement, for his thought and interest was absorbed on one object only, and that was to catch a sight again of that lovely face, which had fascinated him before he was aware of it, or could quite define his real feelings. He found it impossible to advance further into the room, for a party of elderly ladies stood before him, whose ponderous high feathered head dresses, and ample costumes, seemed determined to thwart him, and screen from his eager eyes the object of his pursuit; so there he stood, and was perhaps rewarded for his patience when he heard their remarks—

" Yes," said one, " she is very pretty, so graceful, and elegant, and as fresh as a rose."

" How she is enjoying the dance with young John Hartleigh, is she related to the Hartleighs ? "

" No," replied another, " only near neighbours I fancy, in the same village."

Then there was a sudden movement on the opposite side of the room, which brought a vacant bench into view, and the ladies made for it ; this enabled Mr. Moreton to find his way to the end of the room, and there, as he leant against the wall, his eyes rested on Laura Godfrey dancing with young Hartleigh. The dance over, he watched her partner conduct her to his aunt, presently Captain Cravenfield recognised Philip Moreton's tall figure, and immediately came up to him, exclaiming—

" Why, Moreton ! you here ! this is indeed taking us by surprise ; when did you come ? "

" Half an hour ago."

" Capital ball, isn't it ? " remarked the Captain.

" The room is very full," replied his friend. Here the band began to play.

" Ah, that's it," exclaimed Captain Cravenfield, excitedly.

" Moreton," he added gaily, " I am engaged to dance with the prettiest, sweetest and nicest girl in the room," and he hurried off, leaving Mr. Moreton to his own meditations, which at that moment were anything but amicable or pleasant, as he watched the Captain lead off his partner, and noticed how happy Laura seemed ; and it was evident to him, by the beaming expression of her eyes, she was interested in the Captain's conversation.

Others, too, were watching that handsome couple besides himself; for as he remained there, still leaning against the wall, envying his friend's happiness, he heard one gentleman say to another—

" Who is that lovely girl dancing with the Naval Captain ? "

" I don't know ; she came with the Hartleighs. She dances well—he is a good looking fellow."

" Yes ; a handsome couple. I say, he's over head and ears in love."

" A decided flirtation," drawled out the other.

" By Jove ! I take it to be something more than that ; ring—licence – white favours, depend upon it, are all ready."

" Well, she is the belle of the room, and the best dancer."

" Decidedly," said the other, as they sauntered away, little knowing the bitter feelings their comments had called up in Philip Moreton's heart, angry with himself ; angry with every one.

" Why did he come ? " he asked himself. " What was it to him who she danced with, or what those fellows chose to imagine ? He was a fool! a stupid looker-on! What did he care to see dancing, and every one so happy; he would not stay there another moment, but go back to solitude and cigars.

A rush at this moment to the end of the room made it difficult for him to stir from the wall, and after a little time, when the crowd had somewhat dispersed, he saw Mrs. Hartleigh, with Laura, making their way up to him. It was impossible then to leave, for he saw Mrs. Hartleigh had observed him.

" Oh, Mr. Moreton, you really have come! Then you changed your mind. How did you come ? "

" Yes, Mrs. Hartleigh, I changed my mind, and drove over."

" There are a great many strangers here to-night," she remarked.

Then turning round, she saw at a little distance from her, a friend, and drawing Laura's arm within hers, she said—

·" Excuse me, Mr. Moreton, I must introduce my young friend to that lady."

While Mrs. Hartleigh and her friend were engaged in conversation, Laura looked across at Mr. Moreton, who remained watching her. The expression of his countenance was so unusually sad that she could not help noticing it; and, wondering if he was ill, she went up to him in so natural and sweet a manner, that it almost made him start, as she said—

"Is not this a delightful ball, Mr. Moreton?"

"I suppose it is, to those who enjoy dancing," he replied.

"Don't you dance?" she asked.

"Never."

"Never!" she repeated. "Why, don't you like it, then?"

"I never learnt."

"Oh, what a pity!" she said. "Had you no one to teach you? I mean," she added, "no sister or lady cousins, to make you care to learn?"

"No; I never had any relation to teach me anything, or I may say," he added, with a half-suppressed sigh, "to care for me."

"Your mother, Mr. Moreton—" He took up her words.

"Ah, my mother!" he said sorrowfully, "she died when I was a mere child, Miss Laura. I have but one relation in the world, an uncle."

Laura's heart was full of compassion for this lonely man.

"Now," she thought, "I know what has made him so reserved and shy with us; he has no lady relations."

"I hope, Mr. Moreton, your uncle is not a very elderly man."

"Yes! Indeed, I regret to think how he is advancing in years; and how soon I may stand alone in the world."

"I am glad, Mr. Moreton, you changed your mind, and came here to-night, because it would have been so dull for you all alone at the Three Oaks," she said so simply.

"I am accustomed to solitude, Miss Laura."

"But surely you do not prefer it. Are you not sociably inclined?" she asked.

"Longworth has made me so."

"Oh, yes!" she eagerly exclaimed. "The Hartleighs are delightful, and their house is open to every one, I think."

"Yes, indeed," he replied, "and I shall never forget Longworth and their hospitality. But may I ask you to allow me the pleasure of taking you down to supper? As I cannot dance with you, will you grant me this happiness?" he said.

"I will, indeed," she replied, looking up at him with a smile which made Philip Moreton feel repaid for going to the ball.

She was about to ask him some question relating to his life with his uncle, when Captain Cravenfield came up, as the band begun, saying—

"There is our last valse before supper, Miss Godfrey." And he led her away.

As she passed, a flower fell from her

bouquet. What could have induced that grave, silent man to pick it up, and when no one saw him, put it tenderly into his pocket! He—the last man in the world to be sentimental!

When the valse was over, her partner insisted on taking her down to supper. It was in vain she urged—

"Mr. Moreton was waiting for her, and she had promised that he should take her down."

"Oh, he will guess how it is. Moreton won't mind it, I assure you."

And, in spite of her hesitation, he led her out of the room—as she caught sight of Philip Moreton looking about for her!

Not finding her in the ball-room, he entered the supper-room, and there he saw Laura, seated by his friend's side, who was paying her marked attention.

She, however, could not feel quite happy, for she felt conscious that she had not behaved well to Mr. Moreton, and he would think it so ungrateful of her, after all he had done for her brother, and had, in various ways, to herself and Jane shown so much real kindness of heart. She saw him look sadly towards her, and leave the room.

In spite of the Captain's attentions and lively conversation, she could not help thinking of his disappointment. And then his sad speech, " I stand alone in the world," came into her mind, and made her anxious to explain the matter to him; but there was no opportunity that night, for on returning to the ball-room he was nowhere to be seen.

The drive home after a ball is always a pleasant part of the affair; the stars shining through the obscurity—for it was advancing towards daybreak—the air fresh and frosty.

For some miles they kept up a pleasant chatter. All were excited, and each had his or her remarks to make, and questions to ask.

At last fatigue gradually crept over them, and before they came to the end of their drive, profound silence reigned within the carriage.

Just as Laura had closed the door of her room, where Mrs. Tims sat by the fire, a gentle tap at the door made her re-open it, when Aunt Eleanor entered.

"My dear, I just wanted to have a look at you. Well, you have not crushed your flowers. Had you a pleasant ball?"

"Yes, delightful."

"Did you dance with the handsome Captain?" she asked, putting her trumpet ready for the answer.

"Oh, yes, a great many times—he was my pleasantest partner."

"Ah, yes, my dear, I was sure he would be; but now Mrs. Tims has taken off your beautiful dress I will say pleasant dreams to you."

And in a short time Laura was alone.

CHAPTER VII.

WHAT could be the reason, that the morning after the ball, Philip Moreton and his friend sat so unusually silent over their breakfast?

The Captain, generally so gay and chatty, was quite dull, so absorbed in thought, and so absent in manner, that Mr. Moreton silently noticed it, and took up the paper, but was watching his companion more than reading.

The Captain became restless; he rose from his seat and walked about the room; then stood for a moment at the window. Then he went to the glass over the chimney-piece and trimmed his whiskers.

At last, taking up his hat, he left the room, but almost immediately returned, and, laying his hand on Mr. Moreton's shoulder, said—

"Moreton, don't think me a fool. I—I—I am desperately in love! Wish me luck; I have made up my mind to go at once and propose to Miss Laura Godfrey!" And he left the room.

Mr. Moreton let his paper fall. What had he heard? Words that completely overwhelmed him. Mingled feelings rose in his heart—disappointment, anger, passion.

At that moment he hated his friend, for that moment told him the depth of his own love for Laura Godfrey!

"Laura Godfrey. Fool!" he exclaimed, "why did I bring him here? What has he dared to rob me of?"

He started up! But sitting down again, he rested his head on his arms, and that strong man shook with grief.

After a time he rose from his chair and paced the room, saying to himself—

"I might have guessed what would happen, he, so agreeable, so admired and sought after by every one—any woman would accept

him! Why was I so slow, so guarded, so
confoundedly dull? Why was I brought up
to despise women, and to shun the society of
ladies? Oh, uncle, uncle, you know not the
misery your teachings, your warnings have
brought upon me," and a tear actually fell on
his hand, and this roused him. "Nonsense!
What weakness! What folly," and then he
began to think of what he should do. Stay
and see the happiness of his friend? No, he
would never see him again! Where should
he go? To Kemberton? No, anywhere, but
to a quiet, peaceful, place; he would go
abroad, to the Falls, where the roaring,
tossing tumult of the waters would prevent
or drown thought, and be in unison with the
trouble raging at his heart. A disappointment in love is said to be more hard to get
over than any other; that the passion itself
so softens and subdues the heart, that it dis-
ables it from struggling and bearing up against
the woes and distress which befall it.

Mr. Moreton was a man of strong feeling,

he was a really good man, and had he been brought up under the tender influence of womankind, he would have felt his own natural power to win, and ingratiate himself with those of the opposite sex; but for want of this domestic education, he threw himself within himself, and lost a sort of self-confidence in his ability to please; meanwhile the uncle was training him in his opinions of the frivolity, the weakness, and unfaithfulness of the sex. No wonder he became so guarded and cautious, and was unable to fathom his own heart, until circumstances did it for him, and then, too late, alas, for his peace of mind. He left Longworth as fast as his horse would take him, ordering his groom to pack everything and follow him to Exeter, there he would decide where to go. The last event was followed by another.

"Uncle," said Mr. John Hartleigh, "I wish to speak with you."

"No more Oxford bills, no trouble of that sort, I hope John."

" No, uncle, I have not forgotten my promise, nor your kindness in that matter."

" Come, that's right. Now out with it."

" About my profession. I was thinking of taking orders."

"The Church—eh?" exclaimed Mr. Hartleigh. " Well, you must consider, that is a very serious matter, there are so many points to be thought of, and questions which your own conscience alone can answer. In the first place as to your object. Whether you think it the easiest mode of life, or for the mere gain? Then as to your own suitableness of character. In short, John, you must examine your motives, and sift them thoroughly, to ascertain your real desire for entering into Holy Orders, and then question yourself as to the stability of your intentions!"

" Indeed, uncle, I assure you, I have for some time thought seriously over the matter, and this is not the first time, you know, that I have mentioned that subject to you. If you recollect, last year I proposed it."

" You did, I remember, and I dismissed it, because I thought you were then not speaking with due reverence of the sacred office—the high privilege, I should say, of entering into Holy Orders. It was well said long ago by one of great experience, that ' young men are apt to think it an easy work, and that to be a divine is nothing else but to wear black, to look seriously, and to speak confidently for an hour; but confidence and propriety are not all one. The Divine Office spreads itself into infinite and other occasions of labour, and in those that reach the utmost of so great a profession it requires depth of knowledge, as well as height of elo-quence.' "

" Yes, uncle, I know that I shall have to study and read up a good deal, but I am prepared to do that."

" Then, John, you must be content with a curacy until some favourable chance gives you a living, but as a single man you will be able to do very well on a small curacy."

" I suppose some are better than others. Men *do* marry on only a curacy, uncle."

" Marry ! What put that in your head ? I hope you have no such scheme yet awhile ? "

"No, not yet, uncle, but I hope by-and-by."

" Nonsense, nonsense," interrupted Mr. Hartleigh. " What are you thinking of foolish boy ? " There was a pause ; at last the uncle said—

" John, don't conceal anything from me, are you engaged to any lady ? "

" No, uncle, I am not, but now I will confess to you that I feel an affection for Miss Jasper, and I hope by steady persever-ance in my profession to deserve her."

" I am very much taken by surprise, John. As far as the young lady herself is concerned, I can have no objection ; from all I saw of her she seems good and amiable, but I am afraid she has no fortune, and I do not see how you could marry upon a curate's stipend."

" I don't intend, sir, or wish to marry yet awhile, all I want is your consent to my becoming engaged to her. I have no reason to think that she cares for me. I want to secure her affection."

" But is that right, unless you have wherewithal to live upon?"

" Yes, uncle, if she is content to wait."

" Well, you foolish fellow, I'll talk it over with your aunt, in the meantime think seriously of your future profession."

The Rector no sooner left his nephew, than he went in search of his wife, to whom he communicated the discovery he had just made, and was somewhat surprised at her receiving the intelligence so quietly.

" But are you not equally taken by surprise, Mary?" he asked.

"No, I saw that John was very much taken with the young lady, whenever they met."

" How strange it is," he said, " you ladies always see those things directly."

" Well, as to that, did not you first tell

me your suspicions with regard to Captain Cravenfield's more than admiration for Laura Godfrey?"

" Yes, certainly," he replied, " but that was so very evident; now pray what do you think of this affair of John's? I can't say that it is at all desirable for him to engage himself at present."

Mrs. Hartleigh was attached to her nephew; she was sensible and good hearted, the Rector always relied on her judgment; she thought an engagement would keep him steady, and make him eager to work, so after a little time she succeeded in bringing him to her views.

CHAPTER VIII.

When Philip Moreton reached Exeter, he made up his mind what to do. He had not seen his uncle since his return from Norway, and although he would much rather have started at once for the continent, yet he would not be selfish in his grief, for he knew that it would be a great disappointment to his uncle, to hear he had gone abroad again without having been to see him; he therefore left his horse at the hotel, with a letter of instruction for his groom, and, taking the first train, hastened on to Kemberton.

The old Baronet was in excellent health and spirits, and gave his nephew, as usual, a hearty welcome, telling him he was eager to hear all about his late trip to Norway.

It has been remarked that—" Love is an affection that cannot properly be said to be in the soul, as the soul in that, the soul may sooner leave off to subsist than love; and like the vine, it withers and dies, if it has nothing to embrace."

For the first time, perhaps, the fact had occurred to Philip, that any day death may deprive him of the only object to which from early boyhood his affections had clung, and that he would be left without any human being to love and cherish. It was natural that such thoughts should present themselves to him, now that his heart was so subdued and sad. Unknown to himself, he had been living for weeks on the sweet charm of indescribable untold love, and now, when too late, he had all at once discovered the truth, and the misery he had brought upon himself. In spite of all his efforts to overcome his feelings, and forget that graceful lovely girl, whose image haunted him, his thoughts would continually wander back to that pretty village, to that happy cottage home; the social inmates no longer anything to him, his pleasant visits there were over! At Kemberton, everything seemed changed to him, even his horses and dogs were not the pleasure to him they had been; nor did they come in for their usual share of caresses or attention; he liked to wander about and dwell on his desolate condition. It was with great difficulty he endeavoured to conceal from his uncle the wretched state of his heart. Although he tried to talk as usual to him, and to answer all his uncle's questions about his trip to Norway, yet there was so evidently a depression, a something so unlike himself in tone, voice, and manner, that one day Sir Edward noticed it, and exclaimed anxiously—

"Why, Phil, my boy, you're not well!"

"Oh, yes, uncle, I am."

"Ah, I'll tell you what it is, Phil, it's the black bread, Norwegian bread, that has completely upset you; we'll have an extra bottle of my old port, to-day. Ah, you didn't get anything like that in Norway, did you?"

" No, uncle. Milk is the chief beverage there."

" Milk ! ah, poor weak stuff, no wonder you're ill, Phil; now if it had been the gay captain, I should have set it down to some milksop of a woman, who had caught hold of him by her poisonous darts and honeyed words ! Ah, bitter sweets, that disorder a man ! No, no, Phil, my boy, thank goodness *you* are proof against that sort of distemper, and it's only the black bread, Phil, the black bread that is playing the deuce with your inside."

At this moment the butler entered the room, and told Sir Edward a man wished to speak to him.

" Show him into the justice room ; and here Williams ! " he shouted, as the butler closed the door. " Williams ! fetch up another bottle of port, to-day ! now Phil, that will make you well. We must get rid of that black bread of Norway. He's not like himself," he muttered, as he left the room, while his nephew hardly knew whether to smile or to sigh over his uncle's remarks.

Time passed heavily on with Philip. Sometimes he thought of going to Sea Cove, but then again that was only to bring back with painful recollection the circumstances which made him acquainted with the inmates of that loved cottage; and, besides, he feared he might, on reaching Exeter, hear tidings of his friend's happiness, which he dreaded.

One day, his uncle asked him to ride over to the town of Oldham, on business; while he was in a stationer's shop, he heard some people at the further end talking of Foxhoe, and presently one of the ladies said—

" But what a change is likely to take place there, I hear the Captain is going to be married ! "

"Yes, indeed," replied the other lady, " and it will make a great difference to Mrs. Cravenfield; do you know the lady's name ? "

" No, she is from the south ; I wonder if his mother approves of the match ? "

Philip Moreton did not wait to hear more, but hurried out of the shop. " It is all over now," thought he, as he rode home, and feeling that he could not bear patiently his uncle's anxiety or banter on his state of health, or his sarcastic bitter remarks on marriage when he heard the news of Cravenfield, and feeling more restless and wretched than ever, he determined, as Sir Edward was so well in health, to set out for the continent immediately, there to forget his disappointment, and Laura Godfrey.

CHAPTER IX.

" Oh, mamma ! " exclaimed Lucy Jasper, running in from the garden one morning quite out of breath. " I met the postman, who gave me three letters, one from dear Charles! how delightful ! and one to me from Laura, and I don't know whose writing this is, mamma; it is for you ! "

Mrs. Jasper looked mystified, as she read the address of her letter, for she did not know the handwriting, and quickly opened it, but almost as speedily closed it, and repaired to her own room to read it alone. There was evidently something important to agitate that good lady in her letter; for tears one by one began to drop upon it, as it lay before her. After a little time she read it again, and then carefully restored it to her pocket, saying as she did so—" My darling

Lucy, must we part?" She would not say anything to her daughter of Mr. John Hartleigh's proposal, for a day or two. It had so completely taken her by surprise, that she wished to think it over, and to accustom herself in thought, at least, to the possibility of a change, which some day would separate her from her loved child. When she returned to the parlour, Lucy exclaimed—

"Mamma, I have had such a nice letter from Laura, she tells me that her engagement is not to be a long one, in case Captain Cravenfield should be called to sea, and she is very anxious that you would allow me to be one of her bridesmaids."

"Indeed, my dear Lucy, I do not know what to say about that, for I am afraid the bridesmaid's dress will be an expensive matter."

"But, mamma, you need not think about my dress, for Laura is going to give it to me. She says she hopes you will give her this great pleasure."

"My dear, she is very kind; when is the wedding to take place?"

"She thinks it will be early next month."

"That is very soon; I hope she will be very happy."

"Yes, mamma, it does seem very soon; but Laura says she has seen enough of Captain Cravenfield to know he is very good, and to feel that she is very fond of him already."

"Well, my dear, I will not refuse you the pleasure of going to the wedding."

"Thank you so much, mamma; Laura will be delighted when she gets my letter to tell her you consent."

"Now, Lucy, let me hear what Charles says. Where does he date from?"

"From Malta, April 3rd. He seems to be very happy, and to like his ship; he says he has 'a jolly chum,' and that he is teaching him to take sketches."

"Does he say anything of the ship being ordered home?"

"No; she is ordered to Naples, and Charles

says he hopes there will be a 'blow up' of Mount Vesuvius again."

" Well, give me his letter that I may read it when the candles come," said Mrs. Jasper.

A few days after, when her daughter Lucy had returned to the room after seeing her little sisters in bed, and settled herself at work, Mrs. Jasper unlocked her desk, and taking out the letter, she said—

" Lucy, my dear, this letter concerns you."

" Me! mamma!" and blushes covered her face.

" Yes, dear; it is from Mr. John Hartleigh, asking my permission to make you an offer of marriage!"

" Oh! mamma," she exclaimed, looking frightened.

"Don't you like him, Lucy?"

" Yes—no—I can't tell. I believe so—but I could not bear to leave you, mamma," and here she began to cry.

" My dear child," said her mother, " your feelings are quite natural; you must think seriously the matter well over. You say truly that you do not know whether you like him sufficiently to accept him at once; therefore, I shall not consent to any engagement for the present until you have seen more of each other. I must say that I like his letter; it is straightforward, frank and very gentleman-like."

" Oh, yes ! mamma, he is a thorough gentle-man, and was so very kind to me; but I don't want to leave you, and Clara, and Gertrude ! "

" Well, my dear, you see he does not think it possible that he could marry for some years. He says his prospects are good, and his uncle will assist him, and that it is entirely with his sanction that he writes to me for my consent. I should like to see him, and after a little time, perhaps, I may invite him here; but I must feel quite sure that my dear little Lucy does not positively dislike—"

" Oh, no, mamma," interrupted Lucy. " Nobody could dislike Mr. John Hartleigh; he is so good and amiable and pleasant."

Mrs. Jasper was quite satisfied from the enthusiastic manner in which her daughter spoke that the young man would win his way to Lucy's heart. She replied to the letter which, on the youthful lover's receiving, he hastened with it to his aunt, who remarked—

"I like her letter, John; it is giving you hope. At the same time the mother is right in wishing you to know more of one another before engaging yourselves. You will hear again, and no doubt you will be invited there. She tells you her daughter is timid, and she rightly wishes for time to consider the matter."

"You think I may hope, then, aunt?"

"Yes, I do indeed, my dear John. Remember your motto, and follow it, 'Hope on, hope ever.'"

"I am sure," he said, "I have to thank you, Aunt Mary, for bringing my uncle round. I am just going to run down to Miss Godfrey.

Lucy is such a favourite, that I am sure the news will give pleasure."

"Do, John, and if you should fall in with Aunt Eleanor on your way, tell her I want her to go with me to call on the Pictons."

"Where is she gone?"   .

"I heard her say she must go to the shop in the next village—a walk she is very fond of for imaginary or real wants for herself or others. You may be sure she has taken the dogs; I heard a great barking as she set off."

"Which way did my aunt go?" asked Mr. John of the coachman.

"That way, sir, towards Stanleigh. She asked me (smiling) whether 'twas *too* far for them dogs. Blessee, sir, she's as fond of them dogs, I believe, as if they was Christians!"

Mr. John had not proceeded very far, when he met his aunt, looking somewhat pale and frightened.   .

"What's the matter, aunt?"

"Why, that ungrateful Rover! he has given me such trouble."

" Why, what has he done ? "

" Why, I started this morning for ' London House '—that new shop—and I thought I would take the three dogs for a treat. When I went in, Mrs. Harris remarked how thin poor Rover was."

" ' Yes,' I said, ' he looks half starved; see how his poor bones stick out.'

" I made them all lie down for a rest, whilst she and I were talking about a dress for a poor girl who is going out to service, and we were so busy with quantities and qualities, that I never thought of the dogs till I was preparing to go, and there lay two of them with their noses between their paws—but where was Rover ! Just then we heard a great noise in the little sitting-room, and I said—

" ' Oh, Mrs. Harris, I hope there's nothing in that room that the dog can take.'

" ' Yes, ma'am,' said she, ' my butter.'

" I followed her in, and what was my horror to see the dog had got the basket down, and had eaten ever so many of the half-pound pats. But he did it so beautifully, that there was not a bit on the floor."

" I hope you flogged the brute well."

" No ; I told Mrs. Harris to pick out all that was good, and that I would pay for what Rover had eaten. And look at his sides now ! Why, it was exactly as if he had heard what I had remarked upon them. He has filled them out so, that he doesn't look like the same dog ! But poor Mrs. Harris had packed the basket all ready for sending to market."

" You brute ! " said he, throwing a stick at the culprit.

" Oh, John, don't hurt him ; he really did it so *very* neatly."

Here he burst out laughing at his aunt's simplicity. Then he gave her Mrs. Hartleigh's message, adding—

" But I am afraid your butter catastrophe has delayed you, and that you will find my aunt gone."

" Oh, I really felt so frightened when I saw the butter basket on the floor, I don't think I have recovered it yet."

Here Mr. John, having reached the Cottage, said—

" I am going in here, so I must wish you good-bye."

CHAPTER X.

THE old Baronet was so accustomed to his nephew's sudden departure from home, that his leaving Kemberton so abruptly did not excite in him any suspicion. Philip felt as if every one there could read his inmost feelings, and the desire to be alone, to indulge in secret the deep melancholy which preyed upon him, made him hasten away.

Was there ever so unreasonable a being as a man in love? and one disappointed in love thinks every one he meets his enemy. So Philip travelled on, believing himself to be cruelly injured by his friend who had come and snatched away from his heart the idol he had been secretly worshipping! He quite forgot the barrier of reserve he kept up, that he never even expressed to his friend an admiration for the lady—nor had he shown

by any special mark of attention, the state of
his heart or his sentiments towards Laura
Godfrey; feelings which, though silent, had
increased in depth and power each time he
met her—from the first evening of their
acquaintance; and when the unlooked-for
discovery of a rival in his friend roused him
to the full conviction of the intensity of his
passion, it was as if the whole man—every
power, vigour, faculty of the soul—were
wrought up in that one object. He went
on from place to place, with these sad and
silent reflections his only companions. He
was not, however, a weak, or a revengeful
man ; his hatred, unruly at the time, was
transient, and by the aid of reason, with a
morally good heart, his anger became in time
subdued into sorrowful disappointment, which
showed itself in his countenance, as well as in
an indifference to his usual tastes and pleasures
—he began to reason with himself, and to see
that in thought he had been unjust to his
friend whom, in the heat of anger, he had

vowed never to see again. Then he blamed himself for his reserve—his taciturnity—his want of affability—it was all his own fault; he saw it all now, and in his heart forgave his friend for stepping in between him and happiness. What was there in himself, he thought, except his fortune, to be compared to Cravenfield, that a woman like Laura should prefer him to the handsome and lively officer, whose fortune, though not large, was ample : it seemed to him now that he could reason upon it, impossible ; and yet, argue it as much as he would, he could not get over his bitter disappointment, and though he did not contemplate the constant and cordial friendship which had been so great a source of happiness to them, being turned into cold indifference, yet he hoped that considerable time would pass before they were ever thrown together again. He was too wretched in mind, and too sore in heart, to be with any one.

Time passed on—he had been during the

last three months travelling in Germany, had come down the Rhine, and was spending a few days at Coblentz. As he was standing before a shop window looking at some prints, some one tapped him on the shoulder.

" Bless me, Moreton! Is it you or your ghost? Why, what has brought you here?" exclaimed Captain Cravenfield. "Why, Moreton—what the deuce is the matter? Are you ill?"

" No."

" Why, you look wretchedly seedy."

" Do I?"

" Come, come, my good fellow, this won't do."

" I see you are ill. Why I've been for the last two months trying to find you out. Where have you been?"

" Travelling in Germany."

" Well, come with me; I want to introduce you to Mrs. Cravenfield—she will be so glad to see you. I tell you what, Moreton, you must, indeed, consider my wife an ex-

ception to your general reserve and unsocia-
bility with ladies; but really, I don't like
your looks. Come with me," putting his arm
within Mr. Moreton's, and almost forcing him
along—

"You want nursing."

"No, thank you, Cravenfield," he said,
coming to a dead stop. "I—I have not time
now. I left word at my hotel that I should
return"—taking out his watch—"and it is
nearly time."

"Nonsense, nonsense—come along, you
must see Laura."

Poor man! he felt there was no alterna-
tive—and he must bear the pain and misery
of seeing the only woman he felt he had loved,
or should ever love again, the wife of another.

He would suppress his feelings, and whilst
he was battling with them his friend was
talking to him about some foreigners they
had fallen in with; but he never heeded his
story or anything else until they reached the

hotel, when Captain Cravenfield, rushing up the grand staircase, three steps at once, opened a door and exclaimed—

" Laura, I have found him at last."

But no one was in the room.

" He went to another door, and Mr. Moreton turned to the window. He heard his friend say—

" Moreton is here—found at last—do come, Laura, and welcome him."

He turned, and saw advancing towards him, in a most sprightly manner, a small, dark lady.

" How do you do, Mr. Moreton," said she. " You see, I know you quite well. Don't I, Frank ? " turning towards her husband.

What a change came over Mr. Moreton's face—as rapid as the change in a magic lanthorn—from grave to gay. What could all this mean ?

He looked at his friend—he showed he was immensely astonished.

" Ah, I am afraid," said the little lady,

"that Frank ought to have introduced me formally to you?"

" No, indeed," said he, trying to recover himself, and taking her hand, " you must forgive my surprise, for I had no cards—no bridecake," he said, in a jocose way, and unusually excited, he went on—

" It *is* a surprise, I assure you, which gives me more pleasure than I can describe."

He talked so fast and so much, and made himself so agreeable, that his friend, who took it entirely out of friendship for himself, was satisfied that Moreton would at all events not forsake Foxhoe on account of the lady.

" Come, Moreton, stay and dine with us," as he was rising to go. " We don't patronise the *table d'hôte*. It is very well for you bachelors," he said, laughing; " but we don't want society, do we, Laura," and he put his arm round her waist.

" Oh, Frank, dear! to say that just after asking Mr. Moreton to give us his company,

is rather doubting your sincerity, and taxing
Mr. Moreton's courtesy—he will now hardly
know which to do."

"Oh, yes he will. Moreton understands
me perfectly."

"So I thought, Cravenfield! But upon
my word, I begin to doubt the fact."

"There, Frank," said the lively lady. "You
see your friend thinks that marriage has not
improved you."

"No, no, Mrs. Cravenfield. I beg to say
that is your own interpretation; but if I am
going to dine here to-day it is time to go to
my hotel. I have to give orders for my departure to-morrow."

"Oh, do, Mr. Moreton, stay longer here.
Frank will be so disappointed; besides, you
will do him good," she said playfully, taking
her husband's arm.

"Yes, I wish he would," said the Captain;
" but I know Moreton's plans, once made, are
—like those of the Medes and Persians—un-
alterable."

"No, thank you; they cannot be altered. I must hasten back to England."

"I'll walk back to your hotel with you," said Captain Cravenfield.

"Yes, do," said his little wife, "to secure his return, lest he should think we did not care, even for *his* society."

Now, when they were walking on, Captain Cravenfield was so eager to catch a word of praise or approbation of his choice that it was in vain that the other tried to lead to the subject nearest to his own heart.

However, the Captain, after running on for some time in his gay manner on indifferent topics, suddenly said—

"Moreton, let me see, we have never met since I divulged a secret to you."

"No," said Mr. Moreton, cautiously, and afraid of driving his friend's thoughts away from that point. "No; at Longworth."

"Well, Moreton, I did propose to Laura Godfrey, and was refused."

"Indeed!"

And Mr. Moreton spoke carefully, lest he might betray his secret.

"Yes; and I could not help thinking that she had some image of perfection in her heart—I mean, that there was some one whom she liked."

"Who?" said he, sternly and eagerly, forgetting himself.

"Well, Moreton, don't be angry with Miss Laura Godfrey because she did not like your friend well enough to accept him, for I assure you that I have found the very woman suited to me. I knew Laura Somerville long ago, when her father was Governor of Malta."

Mr. Moreton was relieved, the impetuous "who" had not revealed his secret, and he said—

"I was surprised, certainly; but where did you fall in with Miss Somerville again?"

"Why, in despair and disappointment, and hardly knowing what to do with myself, I went to see an aunt, and at a friend's house in her neighbourhood I met Laura again.

We saw a good deal of one another, and the end of it was that we became attached, and our marriage was rather hurried, as her father wished it to take place before he left England."

"Indeed! Well, Cravenfield, I wish you every happiness, and I think she seems well suited to you."

Here they reached the hotel, and having arranged everything for setting off on the following day, Mr. Moreton returned with his friend to dinner, and in the course of the evening, Captain Cravenfield said—

"By-the-bye, Moreton, at our wedding, a pretty young girl, one of Laura's bridesmaids, came up and thanked me for a cadetship. I could not for the life of me remember anything about it, and I looked confoundedly stupid. At last she explained herself, and said that Miss Godfrey's friend, Mr. Moreton, had applied to me for a cadetship for her brother. Then I remembered all about it, and am glad to hear that the boy goes on well, and likes the sea."

" Yes, Frank," said Mrs. Cravenfield, "you made poor Lucy look so shy; she was always afraid of hearing the sound of her own voice, we used to say at school; but she was a dear girl, and one of my greatest friends. I assure you, I begun to feel quite jealous when she told me she had a new Laura for a friend in Miss Godfrey."

When Mr. Moreton returned to his room that night he felt that he was a new man.

Hope was now before him. Then, again, his friend's words, " Some one else she liked," came across him, and he became depressed, fearing it might be John Hartleigh, and this thought tormented him, and made him eager to be on his way back to England.

He had made himself so pleasant and agreeable to Mrs. Cravenfield that her husband told her he had never seen Moreton so much brought out, and he fully believed that all the credit of it was due to his " little wife! "

CHAPTER XI.

It was late in the morning after the ball, when Laura Godfrey entered the breakfast-room; she was shocked at her idleness, when she found breakfast over and every one dispersed. The butler followed her into the room, telling her that his mistress had driven out, and had desired that she should not be disturbed, and that Miss Godfrey had taken advantage of the carriage to return to the Cottage.

The fact was, that Laura had been so excited by the events of the ball, that she let her thoughts wander on, until she became too restless in her mind to sleep.

What was she thinking of? Did she like Captain Cravenfield? Yes, very much as a pleasant, agreeable acquaintance; but it was not of him that she was thinking so intently,

it was of that good excellent friend of her
dear brother's; she had from the beginning of
their acquaintance admired his manly bearing,
and fine, intelligent countenance, and she knew
enough of his deeds to show her that he had
a generous, noble heart. Until that evening,
he had never spoken of himself, but he had
now told her in a few words, much to interest
her about him. She could not get those sad
words out of her mind, nor the confiding
manner in which he seemed to speak them to
her. " No one to care for me, no mother, no
sister, only an old uncle ! " I wonder who
his uncle is ? and where he lives ? I wish
Captain Cravenfield had not come up just
then, to ask me to dance. I am sure it would
be a relief to him to talk to some one. Oh, I
hope so much to explain my seeming rudeness
and indifference to his wish to take me down
to supper. Thus Laura thought on, her compassion increasing, till at last, quite exhausted,
she fell asleep.

Sweet, no doubt, were her dreams; she

awoke with a pleasing sensation of something new having happened, she felt compassion, that tender compassion—pity, which is akin to love!

Such was the state of Laura's heart when Captain Cravenfield was ushered into the room. Fate had so far favoured him, that he found her alone. Impetuous in his love, as well as eager to seize the precious moments, he declared his passion; she became very pale, but she was not altogether taken by surprise, for certain remarks he had made to her in a pointed manner, the previous night at the ball, had shown her plainly that he liked and admired her, and he certainly had paid her marked attention.

She entreated him to cease urging his love, for she could not return his affection, she would thank him not to ask her any questions. He, however, did continue to press his suit, but it was of no use. She was very sorry to distress him; she considered that he had paid her a great compliment, and, having gained the door, saying she hoped he would soon forget her, she went upstairs, and there re: mained. Captain Cravenfield having left his cards on the table, hastened away from the house as fast as he could.

Laura had not been long in her room, when a knock at the door announced a visitor, and Aunt Eleanor came in. Taking her trumpet out, she said—

" My dear, I heard that you had been down, so I came to see how you were after all your dancing last night. You look very pale."

" I am rather tired. Do you know when Mrs. Hartleigh will be back ? "

" No, my dear; but I see there has been a visitor; did you see Captain Cravenfield ? "

" Yes," said Laura, in a remarkably quiet thoughtful way, so that Aunt Eleanor, whose eyes were wonderfully quick, saw by Laura's face that something had happened, and guessed it all, and silently wondered. Then perceiving how ill and fatigued Laura looked, she said—

" " Would you like to go home, my dear ? "

" Yes, I should very much, but perhaps I ought to wait to see Mrs. Hartleigh. She may think it ungrateful if she finds me gone, without even thanking her for her kindness."

" Never mind all that ; now put on your hat, and I will go as far as the Cottage with you, and explain it all to Mrs. Hartleigh. I am sure your sister must be wishing to see you."

" Yes," said Laura, " and I have so much to tell her, for I did not go to her room last night."

" Then you have not met to-day ? "

" No, I believe I was asleep when every one was at breakfast."

They soon reached the Cottage, where they parted.

" I am so glad you are come, Laura ; I have been quite impatient to hear all about the ball," said Jane. " Did you enjoy it ? "

"Yes, extremely; it was a delightful ball, every one in the county was there; but—", taking off her hat and shaking down her beautiful hair, "I have so much to tell you," and taking a low chair, she sat down at her sister's feet, and related the affair of Captain Cravenfield's offer.

Jane looked rather surprised, and said—

"Poor man!"

"But Jane," she said, eagerly. "Surely you are not sorry that I refused him!"

"No, my dear, not at all; but I was thinking of his disappointment, and I really feel for him. A woman should consider an offer of marriage as a compliment from any honourable man."

"Oh, yes, I told him all that, and I was sorry for him."

"You did rightly," said her sister, "and I hope he will soon recover it."

"Oh, yes, I am sure he will; he has a mother and sister, and a house full at home to cheer him."

She was evidently thinking of one who had no such happiness, as she now knew. After a little consideration, she said—

"Do you know, Jane, that Mr. Moreton, was so unreserved and pleasant at the ball."

"Mr. Moreton at the ball! Why I thought he did not intend to go to it."

"No, so we all thought; but he was there for some time, and I am quite anxious to see him again, to explain why I did not look for him to go down to supper, as he expected. I am so sorry for him; he has no one in the world besides an old uncle to care for him."

"Indeed! Did he tell you so?"

"Yes, and I think he would have told me more about himself, if Captain Cravenfield had not come up and led me off for the dance; it was very provoking."

"But did you not like dancing with the Captain?"

"Yes, but I liked talking to Mr. Moreton just then, better."

"I am sorry, too," said Jane, "that you

had no opportunity of talking to him again. I should like to hear his history, who, and what he is. I am sure he is thoroughly good."

" That he is, indeed."

" Yes," continued her sister, "and I always felt sure that his reserve and shyness of manner at times proceeded from his not having any lady relations about him."

"Indeed he said as much," said Laura.

" And I suppose," said Jane, "that he lives with this old uncle, except when he is at Sea Cove ? "

" I suppose so ; he seems to stand alone in the world," said Laura, "but I hope we shall see him to-morrow, or next day."

" No, Laura, I am sure you will not."

" Why ? " she asked in a hurried manner.

" Because he has left Longworth."

" Gone ! " she said, in a tone of despair, " how do you know that, Jane ? "

" Tims met the groom, and he told her that his master had set off."

"Oh, perhaps only for a short time?"

"No, he said they were not coming back; he believed his master was going abroad, for he had ordered all his things to be sent away."

"Oh, I am so very sorry!" said Laura, with a sigh, and wearied in body and mind, this one pleasure of the explanation she intended to give him, had kept her up; and now she knew that she might probably never see him again.

"Come, my dear," said her sister, "you look completely exhausted, and as if you had been up all night; let Tims make you some tea, and go to bed early; a good night's rest is what you want." And she left the room to give directions to Tims to get some tea ready.

Poor Laura sat spell-bound, mechanically rolling her long curls round and round her fingers, saying to herself, "what will he think of me? I am so sorry not to explain it all to him." Then she began to accuse her-

self for having given ear to Captain Cravenfield's entreaties to take her down to supper.
" It was so weak of me, so wrong of me, when
I promised Mr. Moreton that pleasure, as he
kindly called it." At last she rose from her
chair, and went to her room, but throwing
heedlessly her hat and shawl aside, she again
sat down to think over all he had said to her,
and the more she thought of him—his goodness, his noble deeds, his loneliness—the
stronger and deeper grew that indescribable
feeling which poets and writers have repre-
sented as a "soft torment," a "pleasing
pain," or "an agreeable distress," which
made poor Laura so anxious Mr. Moreton
should think well of her. But, alas, he was
gone!—"gone, thinking me an ungrateful,
unkind, unfeeling girl!" and she burst into
tears, ever and anon saying to herself, "'no
one to care for me,' and I, too, deserted him
that night; if I could only tell him how it
happened." After some time spent in hope-
less remorse, she began to feel ashamed of

having given way to such feelings, and fearing that the redness of her eyes might betray her, she had just commenced bathing them with cold water, when Mrs. Tims entered her room with some tea, saying—

"Miss Jane thinks you better have your tea here, Miss Laura."

"Thank you," she replied, in a low voice, but Mrs. Tims was in a talkative mood, and the news in the village had excited her, so she began with what was on her mind.

"Mrs. Somers is in a fine way, Miss Laura, about her lodger, the gentleman, having gone, and she fears he never means to come back again."

"Why?" asked Laura, going on more vigorously with bathing her eyes, "why?"

"Because, miss, his groom have had orders to pack and send everything away, and Mrs. Somers, she used to keep all his fishing things, and she is so put out at the gentleman sending all away. The groom, he is no great talker, Miss Laura, but he do seem to say his master thinks he have had enough of our quiet little village."

It was fortunate Miss Godfrey's bell called Tims away, for this speech cruelly aggravated Laura's poor wounded heart, already so subdued and sad by grief and disappointment.

CHAPTER XII.

How various were Philip Moreton's feelings as
he travelled homewards.   At one moment so
new, so full of happiness—for he pictured to
himself the fulfilment of all his wishes—then,
again, some speech of his uncle's, so resolute
against matrimony, so inveterate in his
hatred of women, would occur to him.   How
could he tell him his secret ?   What would he
say ?   He knew that he would not hear even
him patiently, and that he must prepare for a
storm, and, in all probability, for a threat
or determination to cast him off.   True, he
was independent of his uncle, and had a sufficient fortune of his own to enable him to
marry.   But, in spite of this, to engage himself to Laura Godfrey without telling his
uncle of his intentions, seemed to him like
acting ungratefully, and not treating his

uncle as he had been to him, like the father who brought him up, and loved him as a son.

By the time he reached London, he had made up his mind to proceed at once to Kemberton, and divulge his secret to his uncle. His groom met him at the station with his horse, but he was so absorbed in his own thoughts that he scarcely remarked even his favourite horse, but sprang into the saddle, and was soon on his way home, followed by his groom, who "never afore knew his master take no notice of his horses, and after being so long away, too."

In the avenue, leading to the Hall at Kemberton, was a fine old rookery, of which he was very fond, and he always thought that the inhabitants of those tall, stately elms and pines welcomed his arrival, as they invariably set up a loud cawing whenever he entered the gates. The noise they made on this occasion attracted his attention, and, stopping his horse for a moment, he looked up, and observed to his groom that the rooks appeared to increase in number.

"They do, sir," adding, "and they are birds of omen, sir."

The effect of these words made Mr. Moreton put spurs to his horse, and presently he was at the Hall door. The anxious look on the old butler's face instantly made Mr. Moreton say—

"Has anything happened?"

"Yes, sir, my master became senseless after breakfast this morning, and we thought he would never speak again. However, he has rallied, and I think now Sir Edward will recover."

"Did you send for Dr. Hunt?" asked Mr Moreton.

"Yes, sir, but master does not know it; he was not sensible at the time. Dr. Hunt thought it was a slight seizure, but he might not have another. The fact is, sir, there were two or three gentlemen to dinner here a few days ago, and perhaps Sir Edward took a glass or two more than usual, for he seldom exceeds his number."

"Very likely, Williams, and that has upset him a little," said Mr. Moreton, as he crossed the hall.

Sir Edward would not allow that he had been ill, and appeared to know nothing of it, and though he was as cheerful as ever, his nephew thought his countenance was changed. He carefully watched him, but found in a day or two that he was as well and hearty as usual, and he began to tell his old "justice" stories quite like himself again. Still, Mr. Moreton thought him not strong enough to be told his secret.

"Ah, Phil!" he said one morning, "I have some work to keep the peace between Jabber and his wife. They quarrel more than ever, and, I fear, set a bad example, for the coachman tells me he was walking along the road with old George, the carpenter (that man who speaks so confoundedly through his nose), and when they

passed Jabber's cottage, the fellow was beat-
ing his wife terribly.   Old George stopped
and listened, and then said through that nose
of his—

"'That puts me in mind when I go home
I've got the same job to do!'

"And I've no doubt," said Sir Edward,
"the women are all in fault.   Nevertheless,
if a man ties himself to a wife, he must stick
to her, and, as Justice of the Peace, I'll
punish the man who beats his wife, for 'tis a
cowardly thing, although I don't mean to
take her part, for I dare say she deceives, and
jaws, and worries him into wishing himself as
free as you and I, Phil," and here he laughed
heartily; but in the present state of Philip
Moreton's feelings, this speech was anything
but pleasant, and he went to the window to
conceal the pain it gave him, for it seemed
to increase his difficulties.

Suddenly, however, a bright thought
seemed to come across him.   He turned to
his uncle and said—

" I met Cravenfield and his wife abroad."

" Ah, poor fellow—poor fellow, and I liked him so much," mumbled Sir Edward.

" Who are you speaking of, uncle ? "

" Why, the Captain ! He has been hooked, hasn't he ? "

" Oh, I assure you he is very happy; and his wife is such a nice person."

" She shan't come here; I'll have no friends of your's, Phil, bringing their petticoats here, mind that ! "

And he got up and paced the room, muttering to himself, " Fawning, fascinating one moment, deceitful, flighty another," his thoughts evidently wandering back to old times.

Mr. Moreton thought it was caused partly by his weak state, and his advanced age. He would see Dr. Hunt, and hear his opinion, before he again made any attempt to broach the subject on his mind. Meeting the Doctor in the village, he asked him what he thought of his uncle's state.

"Oh, he will do with care. Don't let him take any port for a day or two, and keep him away from those stormy justice meetings; in fact, from anything that will in the least irritate him. I told the butler to humour him."

"How long," asked Mr. Moreton, "do you think he will be in this weak, excitable condition?"

"That must depend on the care he takes of himself. If he keeps quiet, I don't think he will have another seizure. It certainly was a slight one; but you may feel at ease if you want to leave home for any short time. At present, he is getting round wonderfully."

"Yes, he is cheerful, and says he sleeps well."

"And," said the Doctor, "he has a capital nurse in his butler. I never saw a more attentive servant. They were all quite alarmed for their master."

"I am glad, indeed, to hear it. Now, won't you come to the Hall?"

" No, not to-day, thank you. I have some distance to ride, and I must hurry away ; but I'll call soon."

" Do," said Mr. Moreton, and he sauntered into the shrubbery, to think of Laura Godfrey, and what his plans should be.

CHAPTER XIII.

DAYS and weeks passed on in the quiet little village of Longworth, and though no actual event had occurred there to alter the face of things, yet, to poor Laura Godfrey's mind, nothing appeared the same; a " change had come o'er the spirit of her dream." She did not, of course, allow that the change was in herself, yet her heart might have told her that it arose from no longer having a chance of meeting in the village, or at the Rectory, or the little Cottage, one for whom she discovered she had so tender an interest. This was producing a vast difference in her usually happy mind—so complete a revolution in all the feelings does the passion of love create; true it is that she attended most assiduously to all her duties. Her visits to the poor were as frequent, and she was more than ever devoted to that loved sister.

Now, while poor Laura was thus suffering in secret from the fisherman's visits to Longworth, Mrs. Somers, the landlady of the Three Oaks, was immensely benefited by them, and rejoicing daily in her heart at the revolution which this most liberal tenant had enabled her to make in the set of apartments hitherto occupied by the gentleman, and almost as many expressions of hope that he might come again in the fishing season had escaped Mrs. Somers' lips, as Laura Godfrey had silently felt in her heart. But weeks passed on, and no visitor came to the Three Oaks.

" Tims," said Laura, one morning when she entered the breakfast-room, " my sister has a cold, and I have persuaded her to remain in her room to-day."

" I'm glad of it, Miss Laura, for there are a sight of folks bad with these here colds going about."

"But I hope by taking it in time she will soon get well."

"I hope so, indeed, miss."

"Pray take care that you don't catch cold, and get laid up yourself, Tims."

"Oh, miss, no fear of that, for I have taken my worroot. I brought a lot of roots from my sister's; she have tooked it for years. It's a fine bitter, and a wine-glass of it every morning would do Miss Jane a deal of good."

"I don't think it would be very nice."

"You may depend on it, Miss Laura, there's more in herbs than in half the doctors going. Now I do wish you would try it, Miss Laura, for I have noticed how pale you have a got, and sometimes I've thought your spirits ain't like what they was. You have got to be so silent like—there, Miss Laura, you knows what I means."

"Oh, indeed, Tims, I am quite well; it is only your fancy about me," said Laura, as she was placing her sister's breakfast on the tray. " Do ask my sister if I shall send her up a little of this," lifting up the cover of a dish. " What is it ? "

" Some trout I had given to me last evening, Miss Laura."

" Is the fishing season coming on ? " asked Laura, eagerly. " I thought it would not be for a long time yet."

" No, more it is, I believe, for such as comes to the inn, miss," looking rather meaningly at her.

Laura gave a little sigh as the door closed. She did not think any one she cared about would ever come to the inn again to fish ; she wished Tims had not reminded her of her disappointment. She could not tell what it was exactly that she felt, but she thought if she could only explain the affair at the ball, Mr. Moreton might not think so ill of her. It was rather a dull afternoon, so she took her work into her sister's room. Jane was reading, so that Laura and her thoughts were alone.

Presently Tims came in, and going up to Jane, said, in rather a mysterious tone—

"Some one has called, Miss Jane."

"Who?" she asked.

"A visitor, miss; he's below. He asked for you, and I said you was very poorly; so then he asked if he could see Miss Laura."

They both exclaimed—

"Who is it, Tims?"

"Mr. Moreton, Miss Jane."

"Mr. Moreton! Why, I thought he was abroad. Do go, Tims, and tell him my sister will be down directly."

Now poor Laura, in her confusion and surprise, had let her work-box fall, and away rolled her thimble, cotton and scissors; and it was well that the picking up these little matters gave her something to do just then, to conceal the blushes she felt conscious that the announcement had brought into her cheeks.

"Come, my dear," said Jane, whose back was turned to her; "never mind winding up that cotton. Mr. Moreton will be tired of waiting. Do explain to him my not appearing."

"Shall I ask him to call another day? Perhaps you will be well enough to see him in a day or two."

"Yes, do, if he is going to remain any time."

When Laura entered, Mr. Moreton advanced to meet her, saying—

"I am delighted to be so fortunate as to find you at home, Miss Laura. I am sorry to hear that your sister is not quite well."

"Indeed, I grieve to say she is not able to leave her room, and she bid me say, Mr. Moreton, how sorry she is not to see you."

He expressed his hope that she was not seriously ill.

"No," replied Laura; "it is only a slight cold, but my sister is so delicate that she sometimes finds a cold trying to her strength. Now," thought she, "shall I say anything in explanation of the ball night; no, perhaps he has forgotten all about it." So she remarked, " Have you been abroad ? Have you come far, Mr. Moreton ? "

" Yes "—and a pause ; "my visit is to you."

She started and blushed ; she knew not why.

" Miss Laura," he said, " I left Longworth very suddenly, on your account. I discovered, when I believed it to be too late, that I loved you—"

Laura's head got lower and lower, and blushes covered her face, as he proceeded—

" But when I found, only a few days ago, that you were not another's, I hastened back to England, and now I am come to entreat you to hear me—to give me this," laying his hand on hers, which rested on the table. She did not move it away ; she did not say a word, but still held her head very low, blushing deeply. He continued—

" Since I had the happiness of becoming acquainted with you and your sister, I have become an altered man. You have taught me to value what I am ashamed to say—but

I will confess the truth—I looked upon as a bore—ladies' society. I was brought up by an uncle who instilled that notion into my mind. You have changed my whole nature from cold reserve to ardent devotion. Say that you will be my wife."

She did not speak, but his hand still lay upon hers.

" Say," he repeated, "that I may call you mine."

" My sister," was all she said.

" I understand; but will you, then, if she approves ? "

" Yes."

It was enough; he felt that he had gained the prize. Silence in some cases is the best and most dignified way of expressing either pleasure or pain. Certain it is that he was too much overcome with joy to be able to speak. At last he said, trying to look into her face, which was still bent down—

" I believe that I shall make you happy. It will be the object of my life to do so."

She raised her head, and smiled sweetly.

" Will you?" asked she, "now let me go to my sister, to tell her what has happened."

" I will," and he rose to go, " but may I come to-morrow to see her ?"

" Yes."

He took her hand tenderly between his, and said—

" No words will express my gratitude when I may with certainty call this mine."

And Laura did tell her sister all that had happened, partly through her tears, and partly through her smiles. It was a mixed feeling. Something had occurred to separate them—a change would take place in that dear, happy, little cottage home, where they had lived so long, and where Laura had grown out of girlhood. Although this event was one that had been Jane's secret wish ever since she had learned to trust and admire that good man's character, yet now that it came so unexpectedly to pass, she felt as much agitated and surprised as if the possibility had never entered her head; still she was extremely happy. She knew she had gained a brother, and she felt certain of her dear sister's happiness with such a husband. She did not doubt his fortune being sufficient, and was sure that he would be open upon that point.

"I think whilst you have your talk with Mr. Moreton, Jane," said Laura, "that I will go out for a walk."

"Do, my dear, and if all is satisfactory, which I do not for a moment think can be otherwise—still as your guardian and almost mother, it is my duty to enquire a little into worldly matters—I will send him to meet you. Which way shall you go?"

"Through the fields towards the mill." In a very few words Mr. Moreton did satisfy Jane: "On that point, fortune, you need have no anxiety, nor will you, I hope Miss Godfrey, think that I am going to separate your sister entirely from you. My wish is that you should consider our house your home."

She thanked him cordially, and he hastened off in search of Laura, while Jane, knowing that news spreads fast and far, and wishing to be first to tell their kind friends at the Rectory, wrote a note to Mrs. Hartleigh, which soon brought her to the Cottage.

" We are so delighted, my dear Miss Godfrey, that I have come to tell you so, instead of writing, and the Rector is coming to fetch me.   When did Mr. Moreton arrive ? We did not know he was in the village."

"Nor did we," said Jane, "until he appeared."

" Well, we are not at all surprised. I saw he admired dear Laura, almost the first day he met her at the Rectory, and as to Laura, she has not been in good spirits ever since the ball.   At first we thought it was the Captain, but you told me of her refusing him, and then we all settled, from many little things we noticed, that it must be Mr. Moreton."

Here the Rector came in.

" Thank you, Miss Godfrey, for telling us the news so soon.   I congratulate you as

well as Laura, for from all I know of Mr.
Moreton, he is an excellent man—a superior
character. We guessed what was the matter
with Laura, on one or two occasions—at least
my wife did," and he smiled. " She understands all the little feminine freemasonry of
love, and, of course, woman-like, she can't
keep anything to herself. I assure you, Miss
Godfrey, her chief interest for the last two
months has been in watching the symptoms
in poor—(correcting himself) not poor now—
Laura, and asking my opinion!"

" Nonsense, John," said Mrs. Hartleigh;
" however, you may be sure, Miss Godfrey,
that he is very much pleased at his dear
favourite's prospects, for whenever he is
particularly happy, he begins to joke his wife."

" And, whenever he is not, I suppose,"
said the Rector, "he is so cross and ill-tempered
to her, that there's ' no abiding him ' as old
Kitty Prout said of her husband the other
day, when she was complaining that ' he
wouldn't do nothing she told him, not mind

her pig, nor keep quiet, and he got so bad
there was no abiding him.' Pray has Mr.
Moreton any profession ? "

" No, I think not; he lives with an uncle
I fancy," said Jane. " He told me that I need
have no anxiety about his means."

" Ah, that is just what I wanted to know.
I should be much concerned if it was not all
right. Give our kind love to Laura," said
Mrs. Hartleigh on going, " and tell her if she
is as happy and fortunate as I am, she will
do very well."

" There ! Miss Godfrey, that's meant to
please me; a little more joking, eh," said
the Rector, as he shut the door.

" Dear me," exclaimed Aunt Eleanor,
when told the news, " how the young people
are getting a head of us, to be sure. Why,
there's John, I remember him in long clothes,
engaged to be married, and here is Laura
Godfrey, a little girl but the other day,
walking about with a lover."

" Why, Eleanor," said the Rector, " it's

your own fault, you know very well, that you
have not been walking about with more than
a lover, nearly all your life."

" Don't, John, talk such nonsense; there, I
do think of all the most disagreeable things
in the world, a pair of lovers is the worst."

" Eleanor, Eleanor," said the Rector, highly
amused, " you quite forget what an ardent
lover you once had."

" Ardent lover," she said, " yes, foolish
man, he would not take no for an answer,
and he had not seen me for ten years, when
he wrote, I believe to my father, but really I
forget now. I know I did not want to see
him, but he would come."

" Yes, Eleanor, because he was so constant,
so ardent."

" Nonsense! John, I did all I could to get
rid of him, and one day I went up to my
room, and made myself look as ugly as ever
I could. So I put all my hair into curl
papers round my face, and then went down
in that state."

" Well, what effect had that ? "

" Why, stupid man ! he said, ' I was more beautiful than ever ! ' At last I begged my father to speak to him, and send him away, but afterwards he continued to write letter after letter; I never read them—anybody might if they liked. I declare it made me very angry. I did not want to marry. I never did, and I don't think there ever was a happier, or a more independent person. However, I hope the young people will be happy, but I must say, I am not quite sure that I should not have liked the Captain the most for Laura. He was so gay and sprightly, and talked so pleasantly. He gave me such a capital recipe for a sick dog, when I told him how ill Rover had been."

" After your butter treat, I suppose ? "

" Perhaps it was, but I dare say that Mr. Moreton is a very good man, and Laura will enliven him."

" He's an excellent man," said Mrs. Hartleigh. "There is something very dignified about him, and though he is so reserved, he has a very good address; it is true he says little, but what he does say is always to the purpose."

"Exactly so," said the Rector, "you never hear a foolish or satirical remark from him, and I assure you, Eleanor, that if you converse with him upon foreign countries and travels, or even the home subjects of horses and dogs, you will find that he has plenty of information, and has seen a great deal of the world; he possesses much observation and wise discrimination."

CHAPTER XIV.

When Miss Godfrey informed Mrs. Tims that her sister was engaged to Mr. Moreton, she did not appear at all surprised.   She had evidently intended it, but was not altogether satisfied with the way in which it came to pass.

" Why, Miss Jane, he ain't been courting Miss Laura, he have a been away these four months come next Wednesday; he have tooked a long while to consider upon it.   Why ever didn't he tell Miss Laura before he went away, 'twould have been better, and whatever could have made him think upon it so sudden like.   There, I watched him, and watched him, in and out here, and I never could read his mind upon Miss Laura; sometimes I did use to think he looked pleasant upon her, but I wish he had come 'afore, Miss Jane."

" But, Tims, he has suffered a great deal from believing that my sister liked some one else, and he came here as soon as he found out his mistake."

" Dear me! Poor gentleman! (altering her tone and manner) there is nobody in the world besides Mr. Moreton I should like for Miss Laura; nor think good enough for her, and 'twas that made me so angry with him for going away all to once, but if that's why, I 'spose, Miss Jane, he courted her in his heart ever so long afore he spoke up."

" Yes," said Jane, amused and hoping that Tims would be assured of the reality of his love.

" Dear me, that must have been a very painful courting, mustn't it, Miss Jane? For he to keep it so long silent, and never spoke it out; to be quite certain she liked him, but she do, I'll be bound. Miss Laura's cheeks will now get as rosy as ever, and I do hope he have a good fortune, and he'll be a brother like, to you, Miss Jane. I always liked his looks."

"Yes, I am sure he will, and that our happiness will be increased by this event."

Here a knock at the door called Tims away. Laura entered, looking bright and happy.

"I have had such a delightful walk with Mr. Moreton. I can't call him Philip all at once, though he has asked me twice to do so. He is so good! He has been telling me all about his different travels and voyages. He doesn't talk of himself. I tried to lead to that once or twice; he fears he is not good enough for me, and regrets being so silent and shy, and he says that I shall improve him in everything, when I am sure I believe that he is perfect," she said with enthusiasm.

Her sister smiled, and hoped that he was coming to the Cottage in the evening.

"No; I told him not to come; I wished to be with you, and I thought you had been excited enough in talking with him this morning. He will come to take me out to-morrow, and we are to call at the Rectory."

" Mrs. Hartleigh came to see me—indeed, I wrote to tell them what had occurred—and they hastened down."

" Then they know it! What did they say ? "

" Of course, they liked it."

" They could not help it, if they only knew him properly."

" Yes, both the Rector and Mrs. Hartleigh were delighted."

" I am so glad," said Laura, " and he likes them ; do you know, he was afraid I might have liked Mr. John Hartleigh," and she laughed at the idea; " but I should like to go and tell Tims myself, it will so please her dear warm heart—but I suppose she knows it."

" Yes ; but do go to her."

" Tims, I am come to be congratulated," she said, walking into the kitchen, where Tims sat at a small round table, with her glasses on, busily working. She instantly rose.

"Dear Miss Laura, I do—body, heart and soul—congratulate you, and he, too, miss. There ain't such another gentleman in the world to please my mind like Mr. Moreton. Such a fine gentleman, too—he will make you a good husband, you may depend on it, and I wish you every sort of blessing."

"Thank you, Tims, and I feel sure he will make my sister happy, too."

And Laura left the worthy old woman, who went back to her work—and to ponder over many things.

Mr. Moreton's happiness was great, although he had to spend the evening alone at the Three Oaks; and could the fumes of his cigar have embodied his thoughts, they would have presented various objects—hopes and wishes henceforth to be laid at the feet of the lovely image he had set up in his heart, and of which he had suddenly become possessed. He would teach her to ride; he would get her a horse of the finest temper and tenderest mouth: to discover her tastes

and anticipate her pleasures; to be a brother
to her sister—such were the delightful
thoughts that he long indulged.

But when any very great happiness or
pleasure is in store, it is natural for the mind
to fear that difficulties and misfortunes may
intervene.

So Mr. Moreton again thought of his
uncle—and what he would say. He knew
that he would storm and threaten to cast him
off, and that he would never receive a lady in
his house—this he had told him over and over
again.

Knowing that such would be his reception
of the news, and that he must be carefully
and judiciously told, or an illness might en-
sue, he determined that he would return to
Kemberton in a few days, and endeavour to
communicate his engagement to him as he
best could.

In the meantime, love—that most delightful passion—rendered him as happy as he
had been previously miserable.

Even Aunt Eleanor received them warmly at the Rectory; " disagreeable things," as she asserted, that all lovers were.

The good Rector would not let them leave the house till they had promised to go there the following day.

" We can't give this young lady up all at once," he said, affectionately pressing her hand.

A day or two afterwards they were walking near Oakford, and Mr. Moreton said—

" Laura, I should like to enquire how Perkins's child is."

" Oh yes ! the boy whose life you saved."

" Yes, love."

Mrs. Perkins came to the door, and stared at seeing visitors, but asked them to walk in.

" Where is your grandchild?" asked Laura. " Here is the gentleman who saved him from being drowned."

" I thought as how it was, miss, but wasn't sure."

Mr. Moreton said—

"I hope, Mrs. Perkins, that you send the boy to school."

"Yes, I do, sir; he is grown such a big boy."

"Does the gentleman," asked Laura, "continue to send the money for him?"

"He do, miss, regular."

"How very kind! Is it not?" she said, turning to Mr. Moreton. "Ever since the father's committal, a Mr. Penhorn has sent money weekly."

"Very, indeed," said Mr. Moreton, amused.

Here a red-faced, blue-eyed boy came rushing in head foremost, exclaiming—

"Granny, I've got a holiday—where's the spade—"

As soon as he perceived the visitors he stopped short, hung down his head, and tried to hide behind his grandmother, who said—

"He's so fond of the garden, miss; the moment he do come in from school he's off there digging, and I can't keep him clean. I'm most ashamed you should see him."

" Never mind, my good woman," said Mr. Moreton, "never mind his appearance. Bodily labour is the best possible exercise for the growth of his limbs; it will strengthen his body, and his mind, too, will be improved by observation. Diligent habits cannot be learned too early."

" Yes, sir; he do know all about planting potatoes and most garden stuff, and I don't know how ever he learned it; 'tis because he's so fond of digging with the men, I s'pose."

" Well, keep him to his schooling; but, above all things, teach him to command his temper."

" Ah, sir, yes! You knows about his father, then; the lady there have told you."

"I think we must go," looking at his watch. " Good afternoon."

" Mrs. Perkins, don't forget all this gentle-man has said," remarked Laura.

" How did you know about the child's father?" she asked, as soon as they had left the cottage.

"From experience, my dear Laura," pressing tenderly the arm within his own.

"How from experience?"

He related the story of Perkins.

"How shocking! Were you very much hurt?"

"No, only my arm, for a time."

"Then you are the gentleman, and not Mr. Penhorn, who sends the money."

"Yes; but he has the trouble of it; he is my lawyer, and a worthy good man he is."

Laura said very little. She was thinking of this fresh proof of his excellence—and how proud and thankful she ought to be at having gained such a friend for life.

"You see, Laura, that in spite of all I suffered in my arm, and at that time, I have a great deal to thank Perkins for."

"How?"

"Why, my object in coming to Longworth was to find out if his mother and child lived here. I soon discovered that the boy I pulled out of the river proved to be his; and here I found the owners of that packet, and (he drew her closer to him) my treasure."

In such happy converse the days passed rapidly on, till Mr. Moreton began to think of his departure.

He had intended, each day since his engagement, to open his heart to his friend, Captain Cravenfield, and to write him; but he thought, as he so well knew his uncle's peculiarities, that he would be anxious to know how he received such astounding intelligence; he therefore decided to postpone his letter till after his visit to Kemberton. He was sure that Cravenfield's delight at the news would be as great as his surprise, and he often thought how much he should like to see his face at that moment.

Philip spent his last evening at the Cottage, for he had settled to start on his journey the following afternoon.

The hours flew too fast for him, and he hoped that there would not be many more partings. He thought that when his uncle was acquainted with Laura he could not help loving her, and that he would make her an exception to his disparaging remarks upon womankind.

Whilst he was dressing, the next morning, and preparing for leaving the inn, his groom brought a letter, with "To be delivered immediately," on the cover.

He tore it open; it was from the butler at Kemberton, to inform him of his uncle's having had another seizure, and that he was very ill; he hoped Mr. Moreton would come as soon as possible.

He lost no time; ordered his groom to get his dog-cart out, and then walked as fast as he could to the Cottage. He saw Mrs. Tims, and said—

"Only one moment to spare—tell Miss Laura I have heard of my uncle's illness, and am obliged to start at once, instead of the afternoon." And he was gone.

Anxiously did he travel on, dreading what

he might hear on his arrival; but he saw no one until he reached the Hall. The old housekeeper opened the door—a most unusual occurrence.

"Mr. Williams is with master, sir. He never leaves him night or day."

"Is he sensible?"

"No, sir. He was taken the night before last, and has never spoke since. Dr. Hunt seems to have very little hopes," and she was here quite overpowered with grief.

Philip hastened to his uncle's bedroom. There lay the old man, his face so changed that it was pain to the nephew to look at him. His faithful servant sat beside him, every now and then bathing his head. Mr. Moreton immediately took his place, and made the old servant go and take some rest. He began to blame himself for not having come before, and as he sat there doing all the little offices of nurse, he thought more upon the past than the future.

All that his uncle had done for him, how

he had loved him from his boyhood as if he had been his father, now came ever before him. What would he not now give to hear once again, and be able to tell him his secret.

This was his fervent hope, as he sat watching the unconscious form. The Doctor entered the room, and told him he was glad he was come, but shook his head as he pointed to the bed. He produced a bottle from his pocket. They tried to raise the patient's head, and placed more pillows to support him, and did all they could think of for his comfort.

Mr. Moreton sat up that night, and scarcely ever left his uncle's side. Towards morning, he thought he observed some signs of life. Sir Edward opened his eyes, but did not speak. It was evident that he was regaining consciousness, and that he recognised his nephew.

Hope soon spread through the house when this change was made known, for so attached to him were all the servants, that ever since the day he was taken ill, they had been entirely cast down. Even the old house-dog, the daily, the hourly companion of the old squire, had wandered upstairs, and curled himself round in a corner, closely watching every fresh movement in the sick-room, and raising his intelligent eyes to discover the cause.

It appeared that one side of the sufferer was quite paralysed, but he was able to move one hand. With this he held his nephew's, looking intently at him, but unable to give utterance to the affection which was evidently flowing to his lips. Hand in hand the uncle and nephew remained, occasionally watched by the attendant, who, eager to be of any use to his beloved master, waited not for any summons.

With some effort the words, " Dear Phil," escaped the old man's lips. Mr. Moreton bent down and affectionately kissed that now feeble hand that scarcely grasped his. Again the lips moved, and his nephew caught the word, " Heaven—hope."

The countenance changed, that return of consciousness was but a flickering of the lamp before it went out. One slight struggle, and his life on earth was ended !

It was a great shock, the cessation of hope in one moment, and that when Mr. Moreton had begun to build upon his uncle's recovery. It completely overcame him, and while he held that now motionless hand, with his head bowed down on the bed, he forgot all else in the world but that one grief and sorrow. All the late events, all his future hopes, were lost in the contemplation of every deed of kindness, every word of tenderness and affection which he had all his life been accustomed to receive from that lifeless form.

How could he love or honour his memory enough ? Much longer he would have remained absorbed by grief had not the butler Williams gently touched him.

"I think, sir, you had better go down-stairs."

He rose from his knees, tenderly kissed that fine old head, and left the room.

The library—how sad it looked! Traces of his uncle's presence and well-known habits were everywhere prominent. His easy chair, his writing-desk, the very furniture seemed to say—

"We, too, have lost our master."

It is mercifully ordained, though at the time it appears an intrusion, that, when death comes, and the living are prostrated with grief and suffering, it is the dearest, nearest, deepest mourner who is called upon to pre-pare those offices of love, honour and rever-ence for the remains of the departed one.

Mr. Moreton exerted himself—he did everything that was necessary. He felt it as a disappointment that his friend Captain Cravenfield was still abroad; but other neigh-bours, far and near, came to offer consolation. The Baronet, though a singular character,

was a universal favourite—indeed, his peculiarities made him almost a county proverb.
His hospitality, love of "justice," and hatred
of "petticoats," were chronicled as pleasant
sayings which would now be missed. The
news, therefore, of his death, brought lamen-
tations to every quarter where he had been so
long known, and many friends, eager to show
their respect, requested permission to attend
his funeral.

We dare not draw up the blind of that
mourning coach, which so closely follows
those sacred remains, but we know that it
contains one solitary mourner, the only near
and dear relation of the old Baronet; nor
will we intrude on the deep, genuine feeling
of regret and sorrow expressed within the
numerous carriages which follow.

Mr. Moreton—or Sir Philip, as we must
now call him—had so exerted himself to do
everything in his power to honour and show
his love for his uncle, that now the last
office of affection was over, he felt the reality

of his loss, and for several days shut himself up, unable to think even of Laura or his future happiness.

The late Baronet had left everything to his nephew, excepting legacies to his faithful old servants. His will ended in a manner characteristic of the old man, with an injunction to his nephew to "attend to justice."

And now, to carry out his uncle's wishes—"to read, before destroying, a packet of old letters"—Sir Philip learnt his uncle's pent-up secret—he had loved, and deeply loved, too. Then came the shock of a disappointment, which he never got over, and which embittered his whole heart and feelings against women.

Sir Philip felt more for all his uncle had suffered since he now knew what love was, and he thought of Laura, whose love and constancy he felt he never could doubt. How he wished his uncle had known her!

There was one thing he had never mentioned to the sisters, and that was his being

heir to a baronetcy. He always spoke to
them of the late Baronet as "his uncle," and
the reason he did not tell them was because
he had determined if his uncle refused to
sanction his marriage, and cut him off in
consequence from the Kemberton property,
he should drop the mere title, as his own
fortune, inherited from his mother, was sufficient for a moderate independence only. How
should he tell them now the doubt was at an
end ? Wait, he thought, until he could be
alone with Laura.

At last his affairs were settled at Kemberton, and he hastened back to Longworth,
where love and sympathy welcomed him at
the little Cottage. A few days after his arrival, he said—

"Am I too late for the post ?"

"No," replied Laura, "not by an hour, and
I am sure Jane will give you up this little
table. There," she added, "is pen, ink and
paper. Now, what does Mr. Moreton want
more ?" she said gaily.

"You, to sit by my side," and he placed a chair for her.

"But, Philip, perhaps I shall talk, and that will be interrupting you. I will come back again when you have done your letter."

"No, Laura, I must have you sit down on that chair; you may be very useful to me," he said, smiling.

"Useful!" she repeated, "what, read and answer all your letters for you?"

"Yes; and read that before I answer it." It was a circular, requesting Sir Philip Moreton to become a subscriber to some charity.

"But this is not for you," she said. "Who is Sir Philip Moreton?"

He smiled.

"Is he a relation?"

"Yes; a very near one."

"I thought you had none but your poor uncle."

"Oh, yes; that gentleman"—pointing to the name on the letter—"is a very near relative."

"But surely, Philip," she said, getting quite puzzled, "you told me you had none. How is he related to you?"

"It is myself—your future husband."

"You! Are you, then, Sir Philip Moreton?"

"Yes; I am heir to my uncle's title, as well as to his property."

"Oh, Philip." She took his hand as she stood by his side, and looking sweetly on his face, said—

"Then 1 am not going to marry Mr. Moreton, after all."

"No, love; are you sorry? Won't you love Sir Philip?"

"That," said she, "must depend upon how Sir Philip behaves. If he is like my dear, good, excellent Mr. Moreton, I could not respect or love him more—do you think I could?"

"No; and Sir Philip is satisfied," he said, looking tenderly in her face.

CHAPTER XV.

In consequence of Sir Edward's death, the wedding was not to take place for some months. In the meantime, those " disagreeable lovers," as Aunt Eleanor still playfully called them, were daily enjoying walks and rides together.

Sir Philip did not forget his future sister in all his kind plans, and one was, a pony carriage complete, in which she delighted to drive about.

" I really must make my peace with Mrs. Tims," said Sir Philip, one day, " before the piano arrives."

" Oh, yes ; pray do," said Laura. " It was so excellent of her to think of it, and I have never betrayed your telling me her secret by thanking her."

He soon had an opportunity, for she ran

out that evening to open the gate for him.
He began—

"Mrs. Tims, I must apologise to you for
seeming to have forgotten all about the
piano."

"Oh, sir, I knew how it was."

"I assure you, Mrs. Tims, I did not forget
it."

"Thank you, sir. Then 'tis coming," she
said, in a delighted voice.

"Now, I am going to ask you a favour, Mrs.
Tims, to allow me to have the great pleasure
of giving one to Miss Laura."

"Well, sir, there's no doubt but that she'll
value it a great deal better; and now 'tis all
right, I suppose I mustn't object, if you wish
it particular."

"I do, very much."

"Then I hope, sir, you wasn't vexed at my
putting it into your head."

"The piano, Mrs. Tims?"

"Yes, sir; there, you know what I means,
about Miss Laura's bootiful voice."

" Mrs. Tims I feel extremely obliged to you,. for I dare say "—and he smiled—" I should never have found it out; but I really thank you very much for giving up the piano to me."

A few days afterwards the instrument arrived.

" Now for ' The Brook,' Laura—the first song that I heard you sing—and I never have forgotten it."

One day, when the Rector and Sir Philip were walking together through the village, the latter made some observations on the fine old tower of the church.

" Yes," said the Rector, " it is very fine. It deserves a good peal of bells. There is only a miserable single one now there, which just tingles to summon the parishioners to church."

" And none for rejoicings ? "

" No, none."

" I am a great lover of Church bells," said Sir Philip. " A good peal would sound remarkably well through yonder valley. There must be a fine echo amongst the hills."

"Yes," replied Mr. Hartleigh. "I have often wished that there was a good ring of bells to tell of all the events sacred to mankind ; but I am afraid we are not rich enough in this parish to collect a sufficient sum to purchase them."

Sir Philip said no more on the subject, but determined that without loss of time he would enquire into the cost and necessary number of bells for Longworth Church.

He told Laura that he intended to present the parish with a set of seven or eight bells.

"Does the Rector know it?" she asked.

"No; but I have procured all the particulars. Will you come up with me to ask his sanction to the gift?"

"Oh, yes; I should so much enjoy watching his good, happy face. Don't you think, Philip, that Mr. Hartleigh's is a most benevolent, pleasant countenance?"

"Indeed I do; and he is a man of taste, too."

They met the Rector very near the church.

"We are on our way to the Rectory," said Laura. "But as our visit is to you, I am afraid we shall miss you."

"No, no, I'll go back with you."

"We won't allow you to do that," said Sir Philip. "The fact is, Mr. Hartleigh, I have a great favour to ask you."

"A favour, eh! Well, let me see," and he looked at Laura, "something about a licence, I suppose."

"No; not that yet, Mr. Hartleigh," said Laura.

"Well, Sir Philip, I think you are a very safe man to grant a favour to on speculation. Now, pray, let me hear what it is."

"The other day, sir, we were speaking of church bells, and we both agreed how charming they were. Since then I have procured all information on the subject, and we were coming up to ask your permission to present a peal of bells to your church."

"My dear sir, you have, indeed, taken me by surprise. How can I thank you for such a gift—not only for myself, but for the whole parish—and I am sure they will be pleased and proud of such an acquisition."

So the bells were immediately ordered, the Rector expressing his hope that they would be set up by the time which he expected to be called upon for a certain licence.

There was a great sensation in the neighbourhood, as well as in the parish of Longworth, when it was known that the bells had arrived ; and on the day of their consecration a large assemblage of guests was invited to the Rectory.

Southey beautifully describes the church chime as a " Music, hallowed by all circumstances which accord equally with social exultation and with solitary pensiveness ; though it falls upon many an unheeding ear, yet never fails to find some hearts which it exhilarates, and some which it softens."

The Rector gave a dinner to the parishioners, for he wished to celebrate the day, and make it one to be marked amongst the village annals.

It was a bright day of sunshine; the air was so clear; when the feast was over, suddenly the joyful bells rang out, their melody and harmony seemed to awaken the sensibilities of all present, the villagers expressing their delight in exclamations of—

"How bootiful! how heavenly they do sound!" while others thought, with George Herbert, "that 'tis angels' music when the bells do ring."

The good Rector, wishing to impress upon his people the important event of that day, addressed them.

After speaking of the stranger's munificent gift, he observed how blessed was that parish which had a peal of bells in its church, how they were connected with seasons and events, how their very sound seemed to appeal to our inmost souls to draw us to the worship and glory of God. Then he reminded them of the office of church bells, how in unison of sound they welcomed in the Sabbath morn, wafting " midway 'twixt earth and sky," a summons to all, far and near, to come up to the House of God, and in one communion to worship Him with prayer and praise. And then he said—

" When our young men and maidens come to be united in the holy bonds of matrimony, and the sacred knot is tied, then will our church bells take up the blessing and ring out, as far as sound can reach, that harmony and joy go hand in hand together, and breathe the spirit's prayer, that the wedded pair, now gone forth, may chime through life as sweetly in unison together.

" Again," he added, " and when death has summoned a soul from earth, then the muffled bell will remind each one of us that this life is but a fleeting shadow, and warn us to prepare for the other world."

"But now my good friends," said the Rector to his parishioners, before their departure from the tent in which the feast was held, "I must ask you to drink to the health and happiness of Sir Philip Moreton, whose munificent gift you are here this day to celebrate and enjoy. Many of you only know him by name as 'the stranger;' henceforth, you will remember Sir Philip Moreton as the friend and benefactor to your parish."

We will not give the hearty respond to the Rector's wish; but follow Sir Philip the next day to Kemberton. When he informed his household that he was going to be married, the news was received with much astonishment, and caused quite a commotion in the servants' hall.

"Dear me," said the housekeeper, the worthy Mrs. Humphry. "How sing'lar 'tis, when one event happens in a family, others seem to rise up, one after another, till really one don't know what's coming. Why, whoever would have thought of a lady coming to be mistress here, and Mr. Philip—I ask his pardon, Sir Philip!—he never 'peared no more than his uncle to take to female's society. I've been here more than twenty years, and never saw a lady in the house. I believe it was all upon the account of that lady who behaved so bad to Sir Edward. Shall you stay on, Mr. Williams?"

Now the old butler, having perhaps acquired a little of his late master's character, had been considering in his own mind whether he would like to see a lady take the head of the table in that house; however, he was truly attached to Sir Philip, having known him from a boy upwards. So that he wisely thought it would be well to see for himself how things went on, before deciding on removing and setting up in some business. The astounding intelligence of the future, made his mind revert to the past, and as there had not been much amusement of late, he enlivened the servants by relating anecdotes and tales of Sir Philip's boyish exploits, and how he had often and often taken his part with Sir Edward.

"I shall never forget one day," he said, "Master Philip was about fifteen, he was always fond of riding, he could leap over 'most anything, not a bit of fear in him; so one day, unknown to Sir Edward, he took one of his favourite hunters, and boy like, he rode off all over the country with the hounds; he met with an accident, threw the horse down, and broke his knees all to pieces. The poor boy was terribly sorry, and grieved so about it, the coachman said he should never forget when he came into the stable, as he stood over the groom bathing and doing all they could, but nothing could do away with the cuts."

"'Master will be in a passion,' said the groom, a young fellow not much bigger than himself. "'Spose, sir, I was to say I let him down taking him to shoeing, now what would you please to give me?'

"'Give you,' says Master Philip, and he turned sharp upon him. 'That and that,' and he thrashed him well, till the fellow screamed, and then the young master went off, pale and angry, and rushed straight into the library, where master sat writing, and I was there doing the book-case up.

"'Uncle,' says he, 'hear me,' and then and there he told him all.

"Sir Edward was in a rage, sure enough, he started from his chair, and stamped, and swore, and seizing the whip from the boy's hand threw it to the other end of the room, saying 'your Virgil, sir,' instead of that. When his passion was over he sat himself down, while Master Philip he stood still, never saying a word; after some time his uncle looked up, and seeing the poor boy's honest face, he could not hold out any longer, his heart was turned.

"'Boy!' says he, 'you have told me the truth, you have acted like a gentleman and with courage; in justice to you I ought to forgive you, and I do, there—' and he held out his hand, which Master Philip he seized. 'Boy!' says he, again, 'never take one of my horses without leave again,' and he never did.

"He had always a spirit for justice, like his uncle. One day he met with a boy teasing a dog that was afraid of the water, by throwing him in, to see him scramble out. Master Philip, who was very strong, caught the boy up and threw him into the pond.

"'There,' says he, 'feel cruelty yourself;' he knew the pond wasn't deep enough to drown him, and he could swim well enough to save him, if it had been. It is wonderful how time passes on," said Mr. Williams. "When I think of those days, and now see such changes."

"Yes, indeed," said Mrs. Humphry, "I

can't for my part think that we shall like a lady mistress; but, however, we shall soon see how we like Sir Philip's lady."

Here the ringing of their master's bell, and the exit of the butler, scattered the conclave.

CHAPTER XVI.

As Captain Cravenfield was reading the paper one day, he suddenly exclaimed to his wife—

" Bless me ! here's the death of Sir Edward Moreton, of Kemberton ! That will make a great change for Moreton, he comes into a fine estate, and money too, I expect. It was said, that the old gentleman did not spend half his income ; indeed, I don't see how he could. He'll be very much missed in the county, a regular character, he carried 'justice of the peace' in his vigilant eye wherever he went ; a good neighbour he was to his gentlemen friends."

" Is he the neighbour you told me of, Frank, who did not like ladies ? "

" Yes, dear, he never admitted one into his house."

"What a strange, curious man! I should not have liked him, I am sure."

"My dear, you would never have seen him."

"Well, I hope his nephew, your friend, will marry."

"Marry! about the very last man in the world to do that, Laura."

"Why? he does not carry out his old uncle's ideas, surely? He was very pleasant, and made himself exceedingly agreeable to me, Frank."

"Yes, he did; it quite astonished me, I never saw him so affable before to any lady. You should have seen him when he paid his visit to Foxhoe," and the Captain laughed heartily. "I had the greatest trouble to get him over; however, he did come, and the girls nearly frightened him away. In fact, I verily believe Bella did, for she made a dead set at him!"

"But how did he appear shy—I can't fancy it—he is rather silent; but still he talks enough."

"Bella tried him in every possible way. He used to sit stuck upright on his chair in the drawing-room, nothing would induce him to indulge in an easy chair. I believe he fancied it would be a sort of want of respect— and he has a monstrous idea of respect—and what provoked Bella was his studied 'by the rule of three,' she used to say, politeness; but in no way could she get him to flirt; he was evidently quite ignorant of the art."

"Then really, Frank, I begin to be afraid," said his little wife, "that he never will marry."

"Never! the last thing to expect, my dear. I wonder I don't hear from him about his uncle's death; I suppose he has a great deal of business to occupy him."

Next day, however, a letter did arrive.

"Laura," he shouted to his wife, who was getting ready for a walk.

"Why, Frank, what is the matter?"

"I never was more amazed in my life. I declare I feel as if I was in a dream."

"Well, what is it, dear? do let me see," and she tried to get the letter.

"Moreton's going to be married."

"Oh! I am so glad! How strange, after all you said about it yesterday. Are you not very glad, Frank?"

"Yes, very, but I can't recover my astonishment."

"Who is the lady?"

"That's another surprise, though I don't wonder at his taste."

"Why, do you know her?"

"Yes, dear! but I had not the most remote suspicion that Moreton even admired her."

"Oh, do tell me her name, Frank."

"Miss Laura Godfrey."

"Oh, yes, I know all about her," and she said very significantly, "I heard a great deal of her from Lucy Jasper. She's the new friend I said I should be jealous of. Lucy spoke with such enthusiasm—quite in raptures of her and her sister."

"Well," repeated Captain Cravenfield, "it is a most extraordinary piece of news, and I can hardly believe it now. Moreton in love! Moreton caught at last!" and he laughed heartily.

"It is a capital thing for us, little wife, to have such neighbours."

"How far is Kemberton from Foxhoe?"

"About eleven miles; but now I must write my letter of condolence and congratulation. I wonder what Sir Edward would have said? I am afraid his justice would have been sorely tried."

"Oh, he would have liked her."

"I believe he never would have seen Moreton's wife, and, perhaps, in his irritation, he would have cut him off in his will. Hang me if I don't think it was lucky that the old gentleman died first, though I liked him very much, and he and I always got on capitally, but I verily believe, little wife, that the sight of a petticoat by Moreton's side would have been his death-blow. Why, I have

heard that even the housemaids dared not to
have appeared within sight of the old
Baronet!"

"When is the wedding to take place,
Frank?"

"Soon, I suppose. I ought to have had
Moreton's letter to tell me of his uncle's death,
but as he sent it to Florence, I expect it has
gone back to Foxhoe. Well, I am astonished!
Moreton going to be married! Moreton in love!
Ah, ha! I can't help laughing at the idea.
What will Bella say when she hears the news
of 'that cold, invulnerable man,' as she called
him, actually going to be married!"

CHAPTER XVII.

WE must now return to Mr. Fortiswood, the master of Roydenhurst, whose marriage has already been hinted. Enraged at Jane Culverton's refusal, and eager for revenge, he rushed into a hasty marriage, believing that if he had a son on whom to entail the property, that it would be for ever secured from the Culverton family. It was not to be expected that such a marriage would give him happiness, nor did he find that being the owner of Roydenhurst was a sufficient guarantee to his reception in the country. In due time, a son was born, and great was Mr. Fortiswood's exultation over the event. Immediately, he set about the entail, giving Mr. Catchall strict injunctions to see this time there was no loophole by which his son could possibly sell the property.

The great wish of his heart being now fulfilled, Mr. Fortiswood believed himself a happy man, in spite of his neighbours keeping aloof.

With great pride he watched his son grow into boyhood. At an early age, the boy, like his father, showed a headstrong disposition. His chief delight was boating on the lake. Mr. Fortiswood, wishing to be near his son, even during his school life, sold his property of Felton Court to purchase a place a short distance for Harrow, where his son was sent to school.

Mr. Catchall continued to hold an influence over his client, he had recommended to him this public school as the best, in his opinion, for "a young gentleman whose prospects he looked upon as first-rate."

Now, Mr. Drummond, the lawyer's head clerk, began to think his prospects were never going to improve; time passed on, and he saw no signs of the promised advancement; repeated attacks of gout, or

that indolence which prefers letting things
" bide as they be," made his master forget his
promises. But Mr. Drummond began to think
it was time to better himself, and that he had
been " head clerk " in that office long enough.
He knew that, at any moment, he could force
from his master this coveted piece of preferment, but then, what use could he make of
that bond unless the estate of Roydenhurst
was for sale ? He looked to the discovery of
this document to give him, some day, more
than old Catchall had promised him; so he
waited on, wondering why his old Gov did
not make the most of a report, which he
must have heard long ago, of the late heir,
Sir Richard Culverton's death, and apprise
Mr. Fortiswood of it.

Then, again, he thought, perhaps he had
told him, but that gentleman did not intend
to sell the estate. So he continued week
after week to watch his old Gov, while that
box, containing the Roydenhurst papers, continued to be the canopy over his head.

One day, having finished his work rather
earlier than usual, but waiting until his
master came in before leaving the office, he
took up the paper, and was about to put it
down again, not caring for debates and
politics, when a passage headed " Sad accident," attracted his attention. He read on—
" Drowned, from the upsetting of a boat,
Thomas Fortiswood, son of T. Fortiswood, of
Roydenhurst, Co. Cheshire."

As soon as his master came in, he pointed
out the paragraph to him, while he watched the
change which came over his countenance. For
a considerable time, he sat motionless, and
remained silent. At last, he spoke aloud to
himself—

" Poor fellow ! his son, his heir, on whom
all his hopes rested ! " Then, seeing his
clerk still in the room, he said, " Drummond,
I think I had better go to him. I see this sad
affair has happened at his new place near
Harrow. I may be able to comfort him a
little."

He knew that this event, although it had not taken place at Roydenhurst, would embitter him against it, because his boy had acquired a love of boating there, for when at home, he was always on the lake. Mr. Catchall was, therefore, not surprised to find his client raving against it, believing there was a doom to all connected with that " cursed place," and vowing that he would never set foot there again, but " shut it up—let it go to the dogs," for all he cared, rather than sell one acre of it while a chance remained of Richard Culverton coming back to buy it.

Mr. Catchall then told him of the report of his death, but he would not listen to him. He was in that state of passion and anger at his " cruel loss," that he believed the bond previously alluded to was uppermost in the lawyer's mind when he told him of Richard Culverton's death, and, consequently, he dismissed him in anger, telling him " not to come near him again."

About three months after this visit, Mr. Catchall received a letter, which having a deep black border, the head clerk guessed it came from Mr. Fortiswood, but whatever the subject of it was, his master kept it strictly private.

A few days after, he told Mr. Drummond to proceed to Roydenhurst, there to make every enquiry as to how the news of Mr. Richard Culverton's death came, hinting that if it could be satisfactorily proved that he *was* dead, his client, Mr. Fortiswood, would immediately put the property up for sale.

" Now then," thought Mr. Drummond, as he left the office to prepare for his journey, " my advantage is coming, I'll take care there shall not be a shadow of doubt about Mr. Richard Culverton's death. I'll settle that," and he did settle it, by informing Mr. Catchall on his return, " that it was quite true, he had been killed at the Diggings, and his will and papers had all been sent home ; " he knew this must be what old Shuff had failed to get. "Ah," he thought, " I shall manage *my* advantage better."

The result of this information was that Mr. Catchall, the following day, sat down to write to his client ; he told him that on *his* part, there should be no hindrance to the sale," adding, "you know sir, to what I allude ; " then having finished his letter, he said to himself, as he sealed it, " Ah, well, I suppose I shall have to do it ; I am getting old, it may be worth my while, and then as Fortiswood talks of going to America, and never coming back again, and the young man is dead, why I had better make the property saleable."

CHAPTER XVIII

THE encounter with the Shuffles' had left a soreness on Mr. Penhorn's mind, which he could not entirely get over. Whatever he did in the way of business since that occurrence, especially for Sir Philip Moreton, was so cautiously undertaken, so deliberately considered in all the bearings of the case, that it was even sometime before he could make up his mind whether to inform his client of a piece of news which had reached him, that the property of Roydenhurst was in the market. The very name of Roydenhurst brought feelings of self-conviction for his dulness and slowness in not detecting the impostor. However, after further deliberation, Mr. Penhorn remembered that Sir Philip was, in some way unknown to him, interested in the place, and he might be offending him if he did not bring the sale of the property before his notice; he therefore sent the advertisement which he had himself seen, of the estate being in the market.

Sir Philip, who happened to be at Kemberton, received the intelligence with surprise, but with extreme delight. To become the purchaser at any cost, was his instant thought, and then, as if already in possession, his mind became so absorbed with the happiness of such an event, that he caught himself planning and scheming for the future. How he would intreat his sister Jane (as he now began to call her) to consider Roydenhurst her home; to take possession of it with her faithful Tims, to superintend affairs there, and do what she pleased to the place, he knew this would be Laura's wish; then he thought how he should tell them the news; he pictured to himself with delight their astonishment and happiness, and how proud he should himself feel to be the owner of that noble place, to rescue the family estate from again falling into the hands of strangers.

So eager was he to avoid any chance by delay, of losing it, that he immediately set out for London, there to talk the matter over with his lawyer, and to authorise him to enter into negotiation at once with the party on the other side. He determined to keep his secret from the sisters until everything was settled, and Laura had been introduced to Kemberton as her future home.

A purchaser having come forward, Mr. Catchall thought it time to look up the title-deeds, &c., and for that purpose went to his office. He took down the box which had so long been a canopy over Mr. Drummond's head; the lawyer turned over the papers, evidently in search of some particular one, he became eager as his anxiety increased, and at last not finding what he wanted, he exclaimed—

" Confound it ! Gone ! ! Who the devil has

been rummaging here?" At that moment, in walked Mr. Drummond, his head clerk.

"Drummond," said the lawyer, looking earnestly at him, "Do you know anything about this box?"

"What box, sir?"

"Why, this box, I say."

"Yes, sir, it has been a shelter to my head a very long time."

"Confound you," exclaimed Mr. Catchall, impatiently, "can't you answer my question?"

"I have, sir, you asked me if I knew that box?"

"Confound you again, have you dared, sir, to open and extract papers, I say, from this box?"

"O, yes, sir," replied Mr. Drummond, coolly, "part of my business, sir."

"What!" angrily exclaimed the lawyer.

"Part of my business, sir," again repeated Mr. Drummond.

"You scoundrel! What do you mean, sir? How dare you to—to—"

" To make myself acquainted," said Mr. Drummond, taking up his words, " with all around me, sir ! Why, because I am to be your partner shortly."

" No, sir, never, I see you to the devil first. Where are those papers you have so villainously extracted ? Produce them."

" Quite safe, sir, and will be useful to us."

" What sir, *us* ! No, sir, I'll turn you out of the office this very night."

" Oh, very well, sir, and of course I take the documents with me ; no objection to—to that. I have a letter of introduction to—to—"

" That letter, you villain," said the Lawyer, interrupting him, " is of no use ; the heir is dead."

" Dead ! is he ! " said Mr. Drummond. " Ah, yes, of course he is ; otherwise we should not be selling. Well," added Mr. Drummond, coolly, " but really it is a pity ; we might have made a trifle out of him. Now let us turn to the other paper, the bond, sir, that's valuable."

"The bond, you d—d rascal; give it to me instantly, sir, or I'll kick you out," he said, stamping with his feet, and getting scarlet in the face with rage. "I'll call police. I'll—"

"Stop a bit, sir," deliberately answered Mr. Drummond.

"Sir!" exclaimed the Lawyer, now choking with passion, "you are a d—d scoundrel. Your audacity, your impertinence, is dri— driving me m-a-d, sir; is cho—cho—choking me," and his face getting white, then blue, then black, he fell senseless on the floor.

Mr. Drummond lost not a second to snatch some faded flowers out of a jug; to dash the water into his face, to open the window, untie his cravat, and lift the prostrate man's head, was the work of a moment, and in all probability Mr. Drummond's presence of mind and activity saved the Lawyer from a fit of apoplexy. He held his head for some time, fanning and sprinkling his face with water; at last he opened his eyes, but with a

vacant stare. He was speechless; after a
time consciousness appeared returning. He
looked piteously into his clerk's face, who
still held him in a sitting posture on the floor.
Presently he murmured, with a groan—

"Oh! am I dying? Am I going to die?"

"Oh, no, sir, you are better; let me help
you up on that chair. There now, put your
legs on this one. You look better already."

"Do I! Oh!" and he again gave a deep
groan.

"Take a little wine or brandy, sir. I'll
fetch some," and he was about to leave the
room, when the Lawyer said—

"No, don't go; don't leave me. I may die."

Then there was a pause.

"No, no, sir. You are not going to die.
Why, the colour is coming back into your
cheeks."

After a while, he took Mr. Drummond's
hand, and said—

"Drummond, we will work together, you
and I, won't we?"

" As partners, sir ? "

" Yes, as partners, from this time."

" Thank you, Mr. Catchall; that's just as it should be."

" We will talk it over, when I feel better; I want rest. I am getting old, and by-and-bye I shall retire, and then there will be a fine opening for you, young man."

" Yes, sir, you have often told me this was your intention. I have worked for you many years, you see," he said, in rather a confidential tone. " There is no one but myself knows anything of your affairs."

" Yes, yes, I know that very well," said the Lawyer. " I shall see how things turn out; perhaps I may give up the business soon now. 1 feel shaken and ill, Drummond."

" That's the very reason why you should not worry yourself. I really can't see why you should not retire at once, sir. I am sure, for your health's sake, it is the very best step to take for your recovery."

The old man shook his head, and remained silent for a few moments. Then he said—

"Ah! yes, it will be pleasant to retire, but there are difficulties, Drummond, to get over."

"Oh, none, sir, of any consequence. The fact of the matter is, that it appears to me from a certain paper, that by a mere scratch of the pen, whenever the sale of Roydenhurst takes place, you may claim five thousand pounds! In fact the deeds of sale are not good unless this document, which cuts off the entail, has the signature of the late Baronet."

"Yes, Drummond, it must, and you see that letter—"

"Is of no use, sir, now; you say the heir is dead," interrupted Drummond.

"None whatever."

"Well, sir, you will be quite well soon, and able to make all these deeds presentable. You understand what I mean."

"O, yes. I do all that well enough."

"If you get Mr. Fortiswood's bond for

five thousand pounds, and all your own pro-
fits, and, if you please, some small portion
for a year or so from the business, why not
retire at once ? "

" And give the business up to you ? "

" Entirely, sir, and the firm to pass under
a new name, ' Drummond, late Catchall.' "

" I'll think about it; you have shaken my
nerves a good deal, Drum."

"Oh ! no, sir, it is only rest and quiet you
want; depend upon it, whenever you get that,
you will feel quite young again."

" Well, it may be so, and perhaps it will
be the best plan to give it all up, and retire
into the country."

" That is just what I should advise, sir, for
your health's sake—a country life."

" Well, I'll think about it, and when I am
out of the business, you will manage it, I
dare say, quite as well without me. You have
been a long time with me, Drum."

" Yes, sir, and it is time to advance myself. Of course, sir, what your antecedents. were in the business, will not affect me. Suppose (knowing all I do) that in the course of time, I choose to rake up a discovery, for we lawyers have the privilege of creating and knocking down obstacles, and foreseeing and looking out for any contingencies—in fact, to dislodge or disturb the purchasers of property."

"No Drummond, no; that won't do— nothing to be made out of that."

" Pardon me, sir, but I think something might. However, 'tis a matter for study and speculation. Don't imagine, sir, that I am plotting anything detrimental to you in your retired country place."

"Why no, I suppose not; but we will settle about the sale of the estates first. You must put Mr. Penhorn off again till I can look over the deeds, and after all this is settled, then we will close our own affairs— I'll think over things."

Now, Mr. Drummond knew that "delays were dangerous," he saw the long-coveted preferment within his grasp, and he determined not to let the old lawyer meditate too long over relinquishing the business, or the work he had to do.

CHAPTER XIX.

IT was June—that glorious month which welcomes the return of fruits and blossoms—when all Nature is teeming with life and happiness; when the pasture lands are gorgeous with the golden cup, and flowers of every hue light up the grandeur of the stately trees and hedgerows, which, having thrown off the shades of sickly green of the early spring, are now in the rich foliage of summer.

The air was fresh and fragrant with the scent of new-mown grass, the hay harvest had commenced.

It was a lovely morning, when Laura Culverton (for by that name she will have to sign herself this day) awoke. The whole village was astir; flowery arches and appropriate mottoes had sprung up, as if by magic, the villagers all striving to show their grati-

tude and devotion to the inmates of the little
Cottage; and so eager were they to express
their demonstrations of joy, that when Mrs.
Tims appeared, dressed with white ribbons
in her cap, on her way to the Rectory, they
hailed her as part of the *cortége*, and cheered
her vociferously as she passed under their
arches, making that good old lady feel of importance; and how her countenance beamed
with delight to see the enthusiastic sympathy
for her dear ladies!

When Laura went to her sister's room, she
was surprised to find her already dressed and
quietly reading. She was retreating; but
Jane had heard her and told her not to go
away.

" How extremely nice you look, dear Jane!
How rich and beautiful that silver-grey is; it
is almost a lavender, the colour is so delicate!"

Then she kissed her, which almost upset
poor Jane's resolutions to keep up her cheer-
fulness. Recovering, she said—

"Yes; Mrs. Hartleigh has good taste, and she could not have chosen anything more suitable for me. I have sent Tims up to the Rectory with a note, and I dressed myself early, dear Laura, that I might help to dress you; for I wish no one, not even Tims, to see you until you are quite ready—and then I will call her."

"Does she know this is your wish?" asked Laura.

"Yes, and she is quite satisfied to wait. And now, then, I think we had better begin."

The dress of pure white satin, enriched with lovely lace, the wreath, the veil, the flowers, each in turn, took its proper position; and never, surely, was there a lovelier bride!

Jane's very heart swelled with pride as she gazed on her beautiful sister.

As to Mrs. Tims, she "only wished Miss Laura could be tooked in wax, just as she had heard kings and queens were done, in

their robes, up in London," which little
speech came very happily at that moment, for
the sisters felt a choking sensation in the
throat—a battle with some tender thought
that came across them, of the sacredness of
the event now so near.

Mr. Hartleigh's carriage arrived, and he
soon entered the little drawing-room, where
he found them together. He tried to be as
gaily cheerful as possible, though it was easy
to perceive how much he felt parting with
Laura, whom he had so long been accustomed
to consider almost as one of his own family.

They set off immediately, and on arriving
at the church, the Rector led Laura to the
altar.

We cannot look into her thoughts; but
while she devoutly knelt there, her bridesmaids gathered themselves silently behind
her, and presently she knew that Sir Philip
was kneeling by her side.

It was not long before the clergymen took
their places. Mr. Courtley was one of them.

It had been a request of the Rector's that he might officiate in the ceremony, and very beautifully and impressively he performed his part.

The moment the service was over the bells struck out.

When the signing was duly over, the bride and her husband walked down the little pathway to their carriage, when flowers without number were strewed before them. But she was thinking of the bells, and the Rector's description of their office—and she breathed heartfelt "amens" to every peal, which seemed to chime forth blessings on them.

The breakfast was very cheerful and gay. Many little sly jokes were thrown at Mr. John Hartleigh, and at the blushing Lucy, who was supposed to be the next requiring bridecake, &c.

Mr. Hartleigh got up to make his speech. He spoke quite tenderly of his affection for the bride, and in the highest terms of the bridegroom, observing that he, as well as the parish, had cause to bless the circumstance and the day which brought the stranger to their village. He mentioned his liberality in many ways, but especially in that which would tell of him far and near—the church bells. He concluded by proposing the health of Sir Philip and Lady Moreton.

We have often said that Sir Philip was a shy man; but his shyness proceeded from that modesty, said to be "a virtue, that makes a man unwilling to be seen and fearful to be heard, yet never fails to make him both seen with favour, and heard with attention, for he loves not many words, and needs them not; for those he addresses know his genuine worth and honour! Such modesty takes the heart, is gentle and irresistible."

Sir Philip Moreton rose. He said, the Rector having so kindly spoken of his coming to Longworth, he would merely remark how many events that happen in the world appear often much like that little cloud that at first seemed to Elijah's servant no bigger than a man's hand, but gradually grew and spread. So the circumstance that first brought him into the village was small and inconsiderable; but how it had grown and spread, that day's event proved. And as his heart was now full of sincere thanks and acknowledgments for the friendly manner in which he had been received and spoken of by the Rector, so was it overflowing with gratitude to his guiding star—to Providence, who, through what appeared mree chance, was in fact leading him to find (turning to Laura) " Heaven's last best gift my ever new delight."

He then proposed the healths of their host and hostess, which were followed by many others.

As everything comes to an end, so did the wedding breakfast. Lady Moreton left the room with her sister to change her dress. We will not intrude on the sisters' parting, it is too sacred for witnesses, but after Sir

Philip Moreton found his way to Jane. She was alone and weeping. He kissed her, and placing a packet in her hand left her, merely saying—" My sister." It was enough, and she felt it was.

The packet contained a locket—and oh! exquisite pleasure!—the portrait of " my mother," taken from that picture at Royden-hurst; how lovely it is, and how exactly like Laura as she looked to-day! On the opposite side, which opened with a spring, was her sister's hair. Sir Philip had, un-known to any one, sent an artist to Royden-hurst to copy the picture.

When all was ready for setting off, Mrs. Tims followed the bride to the top of the stairs, and kissed both her hands, while Laura threw her arms round her neck, saying—

" Take care of my sister, Tims."

" Dear Miss Laura, don't please, to fear about that," and the worthy creature sobbed as if her heart would break, while she watched Sir Philip and his bride drive off in their

handsome carriage and four. As they passed
through the village, Sir Philip was perpetually
taking off his hat to return the bows and the
blessings so plentifully bestowed on them.

What had become of all Philip Moreton's
reserve, his shyness, and aversion to womankind?

" Dearest Laura," he said, drawing her
closer to his side, " how you have altered me !
if any one had told me a year and half ago
that I should have done all I have this day, I
would never have believed him."

The bridal party assembled on the door
steps to watch the carriage, and remained
there until it was quite out of sight. The
Rector remarked—

" That is a well matched couple."

" Yes," said Mr. Courtley, " so they
appear," adding—

> . " For contemplation he, and valour formed.
> For softness she, and sweet attractive grace.
> He for God only ; she for God in him."

" Now come, young ladies," said Mrs.

Hartleigh, turning to the bridesmaids, "you must remember your office—and the bride's request that the poor in the village have a piece of her cake, and I am sure that Mr. Courtley will assist you."

"Delighted! white satin ribbon, paper and the whitest wax! charming!" he exclaimed, as the party gathered round the cake.

"We must not forget," said Fanny Hartleigh, "that Laura particularly wished for all the old Mollys, and Bettys, and Sallys to have a piece."

"Ah," said Mr. Courtley, "the name of one of those very excellent ladies, recalls to my mind a garden scene, when in the midst of some lovely lines I was poetically pouring forth to Lady Moreton, a Sally somebody interrupted my poetical strain; but I forgive her! and to prove the sincerity of my heart, here is a packet I have made purposely for that particular individual."

"Oh, no! no! Mr. Courtley," said many voices, "we don't allow partiality, your Sally must not come in for a larger piece than the other people."

There was a great flow of mirth and pleasantry over the cake, and the evening ended in a dance. The Rector and his wife never forgot Miss Godfrey ; but endeavoured to comfort and cheer her in every possible way.

CHAPTER XX.

THE flowers that decorated the church and
the road to it, on the occasion of the wedding,
are dead, and " the place thereof knoweth
them no more." Yet, have they fulfilled
their office, and have left a sweet impression
never to be forgotten in the hearts and
memory of the villagers at Longworth, who
declare they never saw " so beautiful a sight
before," and no doubt, they will henceforth
date from that epoch, or near about it, the
events which may occur in their families or
parish. Their honest simple way of showing
their gratitude and affection for her dear
sister, cheered and pleased Miss Godfrey;
they told her with pride how Miss Laura's
" white favour " was put into the safest box,
to be taken out and looked at occasionally, and
to be treasured as an heirloom.

Lucy Jasper remained with Miss Godfrey at the Cottage, and it was pleasant for Mrs. Hartleigh to become acquainted with her future niece ; Mr. John Hartleigh was about to be ordained ; but the young people were to wait until he had obtained a good curacy.

" Well, Lucy, my dear, you are an early bird this morning," the Rector said, as she entered the room where Mr. Hartleigh and his wife were at breakfast.

" Miss Godfrey has sent me up to tell you that she has heard from the travellers this morning, and they have arrived at Kemberton."

" Indeed! arrived have they? well, I suppose there were grand rejoicings? " said the Rector.

" Oh, yes," replied Lucy, " there were great preparations for their reception. Sir Philip's tenants went to meet them, and took the horses out, but—" and she suddenly came to a pause, " perhaps, Mr. Hartleigh, Miss Godfrey will like to tell you all about it herself. I may be forestalling her pleasure."

"That is right, my dear child, think of other people's pleasures, be they ever so small or trifling," he said.

"I think," she replied, modestly, "Miss Godfrey only meant me to tell you of their return to England, and she intends to give you the particulars of their reception at Kemberton herself."

"No doubt, Lucy, and you are quite right to prevent our asking you any more questions. I shall go down," said the Rector, "and hear all about it." On making his appearance at the Cottage, he exclaimed, "I am come to congratulate you, Miss Godfrey, on the safe return from abroad of the 'happy pair.'"

"Thank you," she replied, "they have reached Kemberton," and then she read him her letter, when he remarked—

"A very hearty reception, and very gratifying to Sir Philip. Now, Miss Godfrey, I want to tell you something I have on my mind, that I don't wish Lucy to hear until it is all settled."

"She has not yet come back from the Rectory," replied Miss Godfrey.

"Well then, what I have to say is, that I heard a day or two ago, of poor old Sparepoint's death, you will remember the Vicar of Storkford? an excellent man, most fit to die."

"Yes, I recollect him, with his fine head, and long white hair, the picture of one of the old fathers."

"Yes, but what a life he had with that screw of a wife! However, I rather think that I shall be able to get the curacy for John, and the house is tolerably good, quite enough so for young beginners; much better, Miss Godfrey, that they should begin humbly; depend upon it this is the best way to secure their future happiness."

"Indeed, Mr. Hartleigh, I quite agree with you, and I am sure Lucy will make a good clergyman's wife; there is a good deal in her, though she is so quiet; but she is very young, and her engagement makes her feel bashful and shy at your house. She told me she was conscious of being more silent and shy at the Rectory than here."

"Ah, I dare say, that is very natural, but my wife and I like her much, and we think John fortunate; her mother has brought her up to know the value of time. Well, the only thing is, that they will have to be very prudent, but that is a good thing," he said as he rose to take leave.

CHAPTER XXI.

" WHO would ever have expected to hear of a
lady the mistress of Kemberton Hall ! " was
a general remark on the arrival there of Sir
Philip and Lady Moreton ! It was natural
that such an unlooked-for event should cause
some curiosity and eagerness in the county,
and especially with the neighbouring ladies,
to see the bride, whose charms had effected
so great a revolution, not only at Kemberton,
but on that " cold stiff reserved bachelor, its
master," as Sir Philip was won't to be called,
but who had now become " so affable, so
pleasant, and agreeable, that he seemed even
to like receiving his wife's lady visitors."

One day as Sir Philip, and his lady were
riding down the avenue, a respectably dressed
man passed them.   Sir Philip turned to look
at him, saying—

" I suppose he is a candidate for the under bailiff's place."

When they returned from their ride, the butler, our old friend Mr. Williams, said, " a man wished to speak to his master." Sir Philip desired him to be sent into the library. A grey-headed man advanced holding a letter out, saying—

" Will your honour read this ? "

Sir Philip took it, and looking more closely into the man's face, he exclaimed—

" Perkins ! "

" It is your honour ; but before you speak to me, will your honour please to read this."

Sir Philip withdrew to the window, and read two letters. When he had carefully perused them, he held out his hand, saying—

" Perkins, you have earned this."

The man grasped his hand, and would hardly let it go ; then rubbing away the fast falling tears, said—

" In the dead of the night, when my wicked companions slept, I rose and prayed, and

thought of your words, your honour, ' be firm
to the end,' but daylight scarce dawned, when
all my fearful fiery trials, day after day 'most
killed me. I thank God, sir, I conquered.
I have been out of prison discipline the last
year and more, your honour; but perhaps,"
pointing to the two letters in Sir Philip's hand,
" the governor has told you there."

" Yes, he has, and that you have been for
some time employed in his service; all he
says, is very creditable to you, Perkins, and
this letter tells me that the clergyman offers
to take you into his service if you like to
return."

" He did so, your honour, but—" there
was a pause, " Sir Philip said—"

" You wish to stay in England ? "

" I do, to be a father to my boy."

" Well, Perkins, you are quite right, have
you seen him ? "

" No, sir, the wish to show myself to you,
the man, and not the villain you remember

me, was burning out my heart, your honour."

"Let the past be forgotten," Sir Philip said kindly, " the brightness of the future will throw all that into the shade, Perkins. Come, I see you would like to be in my service."

" That, your honour, is my wish by day and by night."

"Then I will speak to my steward, and hear what situation he will be able to give you ; in the meantime go and see your child, and mother, and I will give you a letter to the Rector of Longworth, to tell him about you."

Perkins gratefully thanked his benefactor, and left the library.

"Why, dear Philip," said Laura, when he came into the drawing-room, " who have you had so long with you ? "

" There, my love (giving her the letters) read them, they will give you pleasure."

" Oh, Perkins ! I am so glad, for now his

poor old mother will be happy again. Won't
you take him back, Philip?"

"Yes, I have settled it all with him, but he
is now going to see his family at Longworth."

"Has he not seen them yet?"

"No, he had a great desire to see me first,
and there I think he showed right feeling."

"Yes, and I dare say he feels a happier,
and a better man already," replied Laura,
"will he go to the Rectory?"

"He will," said Sir Philip, "for I am now
going to re-instate him in the good Rector's
favour."

CHAPTER XXII.

" LAWYERS are the most tiresome men in the
world, they certainly teach one the value of
patience," thought Sir Philip, who began to
fear, by the delay, some unforeseen obstacle
in the purchase of Roydenhurst. At last,
however, the deeds and parchments arrived,
and when duly signed and sealed, were
delivered to the custody of his lawyer, Mr.
Penhorn. Sweet is the secret which is to
give pleasure and happiness, and long had
Sir Philip dwelt on the one which he had to
divulge ; it was a great satisfaction to him
to hear from his lawyer, that in consequence
of the late owner having resided so seldom
at Roydenhurst, the furniture remained much
in the same state as it was on the late Baronet's
death.

" Laura, my dear, would you like to pay

a visit to Roydenhurst?" asked Sir Philip,
and he watched her countenance of astonishment, as she looked up from her work, and
replied—

" Why, Philip! What do you mean ? "

He repeated his question, adding—

" Do you think that you shall remember
the old place again ? "

" Oh, yes ! unless it has been very much
altered. But what could have put Roydenhurst into your head ? "

" Well, I don't know ; thinking, I suppose,
of the owner."

" But do you know him ? "

" Yes, very well."

" How very strange," she remarked.
" Then, has he given us an invitation ? " she
asked.

" My dear, I know him so well, that I have
only to write and say I am coming, and intend to bring my wife."

" Do you really, then, know the possessor
of Roydenhurst so intimately ? Then, do let

us go," she said, eagerly, "and before dear Jane comes to us, because it will be so delightful to tell her about our dear old home, and I won't even tell her that we are going; it will be such a surprise to her." Then pausing a moment, she added, "No, I won't go there. I did not know, Philip, that you were in any way acquainted with that dreadful Mr. Fortiswood. I do not wish ever to meet him."

"No, my dear Laura, I am not acquainted, as you say, with that 'dreadful Mr. Fortiswood.' He is not the owner of Roydenhurst now; he has sold the property."

"Sold it! O, then, he must have heard of my brother Richard's death."

"Yes, he had, and, I believe, was glad to get rid of a place he never seemed to like."

"Then a friend of yours has purchased it! That is delightful! O, yes, do let us go; write to your friend at once, Philip, and say we are coming," and she became quite excited, asking him when they could go, and begging him not to delay a post to propose their visit.

"Well, Laura," he replied, "I have business to do in London, which will detain me a day or two. After that, we will proceed to Roydenhurst, leaving this on Monday next."

"Delightful! delightful!" she exclaimed. "I can hardly believe it is true. Are you really now in earnest, dear Philip?"

"Yes, my love, quite, and we won't, as you say, tell Jane anything about our journey."

"No, unless—O, how astonished she would be, if I wrote to her from Roydenhurst!"

"Yes; that you can do, certainly."

It was early in September when Sir Philip and his wife were travelling on to Roydenhurst; autumnal tints, in varied shades of brown to golden hues, had just begun to mark the season, while fields of stubble and some newly ploughed, here and there, told of the harvest having been gathered in. A carriage was waiting at the station to take them on, and now, as they drove along, Laura became more and more excited. At last she exclaimed—

" O, Philip, you have never told me the name of your friend ! " A covey of partridges flew from behind the hedge so suddenly, that her attention was called to them. " What a large number, is it not ? " she said.

" Yes, there must be first-rate shooting here," he remarked.

Just at this moment the carriage turned a bend in the road, and Roydenhurst, standing on, what appeared at that distance, a high eminence, appeared in view.

" O, there it is, Roydenhurst ! You dear, lovely old place ; how beautiful it is, Philip ! " and she became all eagerness to recognise what she could remember, while her husband sat quietly by her side, enchanted with her enthusiastic delight. They were approaching the park now, when suddenly she exclaimed, " O, look ; how well I can remember that dell, and the quantities of bluebells and daffodils I used to gather there, and that cluster of pines. But, O, there is that dear old oak still stretching out its huge arms ' to welcome us home,' as I used to say, whenever we came back from a drive." They had now arrived at the entrance gate, when she again exclaimed, " O, look, Philip ; here are the fierce-looking old griffins. Do you know I really can remember when I believed that their great eyes followed me, and I was quite afraid of them ! And, yes, there is the little path to my garden. Oh, how dear Jane will like to hear about all these things."

"It is a beautiful place, certainly," said he. " Now we shall soon come to the door."

" Is the lady a nice person ? " enquired Laura. " Shall I be able to ask her to allow me to run about the place alone one day ? "

" Certainly, my love. She is a very charming person ; you will like her very much."

" What is the owner like ? Is he a pleasant man ? I hope he is what the master of this place should be," said Laura.

" He is rather morose."

" Then I am sure I shall not like him !
But here we are. Oh ! Philip," and as she
stood in the hall, she whispered, " I suppose
I must not stay to look about me now ? "

" No, dear," he said, taking her hand, and
leading her on, " I must introduce you to the
lady of the house."

They followed the servant, who opened the
door of the drawing-room.

" No one here," she half whispered. " I
don't well remember this room," and she sat
down ; but she presently rose to look at a
picture, and led on by intense interest, she
was now going from one to another, while
Sir Philip stood with his back to the fire,
supremely happy, silently watching her. So
absorbed was she in the pictures, that she
quite forgot time, until she suddenly became
aware of it, and crossing the room to Sir
Philip, she placed her hands on his arm, and
in a low voice, said, " How very long the
lady of the house is coming. Oh, I forget,

did you tell me her name? What is it? I want to ask her to let me see my mother's room."

Sir Philip put his arm round her waist, and drew her gently up to a magnificent mirror between the windows, and said—

"The lady of Roydenhurst is here already. Allow me to introduce you to her, Lady Moreton herself!"

"Philip! Philip, what—what do you mean?"

"Why, my darling Laura, that I am the purchaser of Roydenhurst; I am the present owner."

She threw her arms round his neck, while he kissed away the tears of joy which now fell fast. After a little time she looked up in his face, and said—

"Philip, this is like a fairy tale; but are you in earnest? Is Roydenhurst your very own?"

"Do you doubt me?" he said, looking at her fondly.

"No; but it is such a wonderful surprise! I can't understand it. Is it, then, *all* yours, dear Philip, the land, as well as this house?"

"Yes, all, quite and entirely my own."

"Oh! how very, very happy Jane will be; how I wish she was here now."

Sir Philip led her on to the door of a small *boudoir*, which he opened, and in another moment the sisters were in each other's arms!

Sir Philip retired to the library, overcome with emotions of gratitude that he had been so blessed, and chosen to promote the happiness of others. Gratitude! of all the graces, the one to be most encouraged; it does away with pride, and takes us out of narrow-minded self. He was roused from his musings by a voice saying—

"Oh, where is Philip? He must see our happiness."

And before long he was sitting with one arm round his wife, and the other round Jane.

"But, do tell me how you managed it,"

said Laura, her beautiful eyes still showing tears of joy.

" Well, that letter you so indignantly saw sealed up for Jane let her into the secret, and Mrs. Tims, too."

" Oh ! dear Tims—is she here ? "

At that moment came a knock at the door.

" It is Tims herself," said Laura, and she ran to meet her, and kissed her affectionately.

" Dear Miss Laura, how thankful I am to live to see this blessed day ! "

Here Sir Philip advanced and shook hands with her, saying—

" How do you do, Mrs. Tims ? I hope you think your lady looks well."

" Oh, sir," curtseying, " she do look quite bootiful—and so rosy."

" Yes, Tims," said Laura, " you see what good care Sir Philip has taken of me."

" Well, he have indeed, miss. Please excuse me—I never can mind it—Miss Laura comes so natural like—but there, you knows what I means, my Lady."

" I do, Tims, and that you will like to take my bonnet and shawl away. I have so much to say to my dear sister."

" No doubt but what you have, my Lady, and it does my old heart good to see you both together again." So saying, she left the room.

It would be impossible to describe the happiness of the sisters. Each day seemed to bring back some recollection, some interest, in an old, half-forgotten face among the villagers, who came up to the house to welcome back the members of the old family, and here Sir Philip passed the autumn, becoming more and more enchanted with Roydenhurst, so adorned by Nature's gifts of hill and dale, woods and lakes. How could such a place be otherwise than enjoyable ?

His chief pleasure, however, was watching the sisters, who were never tired of roaming about their old haunts, and relating to him reminiscences of the place and people to interest him in everything concerning their past life.

Sometimes he would be taken to see a tree or a spot marked by some boyish exploit of their dear brother ; and how often they were now reminded of that lost brother ; how his dream of life, in that journal history, some day to return to his native land and redeem his birthright, occurred to their minds, and was, when alone together, their constant theme, invariably ending in expressions of gratitude, praise, and admiration of Sir Philip's character and goodness.

CHAPTER XXIII.

AN amiable curiosity makes us eager to know, on revisiting a well-remembered place, after any lapse of time, what has become of old acquaintances; what changes have been made in our once familiar haunts; who of the old are living, and who of the young have married.

Two years have passed over the little village of Longworth, during which time events have occurred, some of trivial, some of lasting importance.

The Rector, having secured the curacy of Storkford for his nephew, John Hartleigh, Mrs. Jasper had given her consent to her daughter's marriage; but while the Vicarage, which, in old Mr. Sparepoint's time, had been allowed to fall into a dilapidated state, was being rebuilt, the youthful pair are now settled at Rose Cottage.

The return of Perkins to his native place, his story of Sir Philip Moreton's acts of kindness, and all he had done for him, could not fail to increase, if possible, the respect and admiration for one, whose motto all agreed should be, " Deeds, not words."

Mrs. Somers, having made a " comfortable little fortune," has retired from the business and bustle of the Three Oaks, and is in the full enjoyment of a cottage that she had purchased with the savings which the liberality of the " Gentleman Fisherman " had enabled her to make.

And now we must bid farewell to Longworth to enquire what has become of Mr. Drummond, with his speculations, his boasted " privileges, as the *bonâ fide* lawyer, to dislodge, eject, to threaten with law, the purchasers of property ! "

" Drummond, Solicitor, late Catchall," stood out in large letters on a brass plate in the centre of his door, showing that he had succeeded to the business.

His clerks are perched at their desks, while Mr. Drummond has at this moment retired within his own sacred sanctum, to ponder over his speculations, for he believed the time had come at last to work them out.

That bond and letter, which we have already seen, he took out of their secret places of security, and read them over—

"Now, then, 'my advantage is coming.' Look out, Shuff, for a slice; you deserve it, old boy. And though the ocean is between us, you shall have it."

After this soliloquy he sat down and wrote a letter, but the composition not pleasing him, he tore it up, and walked softly into his office to see if his clerks were idling.

One of them gave him a letter, which he found was to call him out of town for a day or two the following morning.

He therefore again sat down to write his letter, which this time appeared to satisfy him, for he deliberately sealed it, and, putting on his hat, he walked away to leave it himself at Bryant's Court.

"Ah," he said "I wonder how old 'Slow Coach' will like that!"

Mr. Penhorn after reading this letter, looked as if some personal calamity of a most awful nature had happened to him. He became deadly pale. Again he read it, and this time in a low, mumbling voice, as if to be sure the words following were before him—

"SIR,—Perhaps you are not aware that I have lately succeeded to the late Mr. Catchall's business. On looking over documents relating to the Roydenhurst property, I have made a discovery in the deed of sale, which, I believe, will prove, without a doubt, that sale to be illegal, and that the purchase by your client can be set aside.

"I am, Sir,

"Yours faithfully,

"THOMAS DRUMMOND."

Mr. Penhorn took off his glasses and wiped them, slowly; thinking all the time what steps he should take with regard to this strange letter.

Ever since the " Shuffles' deception " he had been in a suspicious frame of mind, and now he asked himself—

" Is this another fraud, another trick to be played upon me ? "

One thing he determined not to do, and that was, acknowledge it. He would this time act with the greatest caution, and not commit himself in any way. After taking a copy, he despatched the original to his client, at Kemberton Hall, without making any comment on the communication. It was fortunate that Sir Philip was alone in his library when he received it and read the contents, for his anger and indignation were roused.

" Confound these lawyers ! " he exclaimed. " What the deuce are they up to now ?"

That it was an attempt to extort money by

threatening him with legal proceedings, he
had not the slightest doubt ; and he thought
the best way would be to treat the letter with
contempt, and not notice it at all.   Still, he
felt annoyed by it, and the more so, when
he thought of the "impostors," with their
lying, detestable papers, which he remembered Penhorn saying were so cleverly done
that some lawyer must have had the finger-
ing of them; "and some rascally lawyer is at
the bottom of this," he said to himself, as he
tossed the letter away.

"He thinks to extort money out of me.
Ah, he'll find I am not so easily frightened at
a lawsuit."

Sir Philip then left the room to go in
search of his wife, intending to tell her of the
annoying letter ; but before he had gone half
way across the hall, he suddenly stopped. An
idea had occurred to him. Supposing this
rascally lawyer, finding no notice taken of
his letter, should have the effrontery to go to
Roydenhurst and demand an interview with

Jane, who resided there, mistress of the place—the very possibility that she might in any way be annoyed by this man—made him retrace his steps to the library, where he sat down and wrote a few lines to Mr. Penhorn, to say he would call upon him in a day or two, in reference to the letter he had sent him.

He merely told Laura that he was going to town on business, and he thought he should go on to Roydenhurst and bring Jane back with him; and this he proposed, not liking the idea of any chance annoying letter or reports reaching her.

It was a cold, damp day when he set out for his journey, and on arriving in London, the fog was so dense that it was with difficulty he could get a cab to take him to Bryant's Court.

On enquiring for Mr. Penhorn, the boy told him his master was out, but he expected him in every moment; would the gentleman like to wait?

Sir Philip said he would do so, and accordingly he walked into that dingy little room he knew so well, darker and more dusky than ever now by the fog, which in London so insiduously penetrates and throws a mist before everything.

Sir Philip had fairly advanced into the room before he was aware any one was there but himself, and he was about to seat himself when he noticed, lounging on the sofa, another client, also waiting for Mr. Penhorn, who, startled by the entrance of some one, was about to rise, when Sir Philip said—

" Pray, don't disturb yourself, sir," and walked to the window, where he stood a considerable time, looking out for Mr. Penhorn, anxious to be the first to speak to him.

The stranger who had been eyeing him, at length rose, and advanced towards him, saying—

" Pardon me, sir, but do I see, am I addressing myself to—Mr. Moreton ? "

Sir Philip turned sharply round, at the sound of the man's voice, and somewhat sternly replied—

"I am Sir Philip Moreton, sir."

"I thought so; but I see you have no recollection of me! you do not in the shattered frame before you recognise him whose life, whose character you saved, you do not know me—I am Richard Culverton!"

Sir Philip started a few steps backward, and stared at the man, but never spoke a word.

"Yes, well may you doubt, and gaze at me; but you see before you Richard Culverton!"

"Good heavens!" exclaimed Sir Philip, "who are you?"

"Ah, I was afraid of it—I—I see you cannot recognise me."

Sir Philip going nearer to him, and looking earnestly into his face, said—

"Is it possible? are you! Yes, I am sure it is," and, seizing his hand, grasped it eagerly,

saying—" My good fellow, then are you alive,
after all ? "

The stranger, still holding Sir Philip's hand
within his, said—

" Yes, and you are Moreton, the only friend
I ever had."

A fit of coughing prevented his speaking
for some little time, when Sir Philip observing
how ill and exhausted he appeared, led him
to the sofa, saying—

" Let us sit down, Culverton."

Presently he was sufficiently recovered to
say—

" Moreton, you thought me dead, and I
wished to keep you in that belief until I had
in some way or other proved to you my
gratitude ;" he paused and sighed heavily.

" Yes, Culverton, it was believed you were
dead ; it was reported that you had been
murdered ! "

" And so, indeed, I was, very nearly ; it was
a miracle that I escaped. One of my companions was killed, and the other escaped,

while I was wounded and roughly handled;
the assassins thought they had left me a dead
man, but after I recovered consciousness, I
crawled to a little stream which was for-
tunately near, and—"

Here Sir Philip seeing that it was pain to
him to go on, said—

"Well, never mind all that, we won't now
talk over that time; but Culverton, what
about your will, how was it you let us claim
the money ?"

"Purposely," he replied. "I wished to
be thought dead, and I was dead to my native
soil, to kindred and friends, for Moreton, the
vow I made was sacred; never to let my
existence be known, as long as I had no
power to get back my birthright, and while
my estate was in that fellow Fortiswood's
grasp, I should have clung to my vow; but
by a most extraordinary cir—" a paroxysm
of coughing seized him.

"Can I get you anything to relieve your
cough?" asked Sir Philip.

" No, I shall be better soon," and after a little time he continued, " by a most extraordinary circumstance I made a discovery, and to fathom the truth of it, I have come to England, and I will sacrifice every shilling of my fortune to do so, but should I fail in my object, Moreton, I will go back to die in that foreign land; no one but yourself will know of my existence, mind that, Moreton, and there my name is Jackson."

" But what was the discovery you allude to ? " asked Sir Philip.

" That my father had left a letter to be given to me after his death, the contents of which was, that he had made a proviso in the deed of sale which would give me the power to redeem the property within twenty-five years of his death; it wants some years to that yet. Moreover, I was told by the same persons my signature was wanting to the document. Moreton! I shall want your help how to proceed. My first object is to get a sight of that letter."

"Yes, yes," replied Sir Philip, eagerly, "but do you know the people who told you all this? can you rely on their veracity?"

"Yes, and their statement threw me into the greatest excitement and impatience to catch the mail steamer about to leave Melbourne for England."

"Had you recovered from the assassin's attack before you left Australia?"

"No, I never shall, but I was better; Moreton, I am a rich man, though I have had to toil and battle with hardships and dangers, such as few men have lived through; but the one hope gave me nerve and energy, and now," he added, with a deep sigh, "I fear all my gains and wealth will be swamped in law; for I expect the fellow, whoever he may be, who has the property now, will dispute my claim, and give a deal of money to the lawyers."

"Then don't you know who has the estate now?"

"No, I have seen no one since I arrived in

England only two days ago; finding the lawyer I was referred to out of town, I came here to see your man of business, and to ask for your address, for you must prove my identity, or they will never believe I am Sir Richard Culverton."

"There is no fear of that," replied Sir Philip; "but I want to hear more about the people who told you all this. How did you happen to fall in with them?"

"I had left Melbourne for a considerable time, going to New Zealand, and to various places; at last, partly from a desire to ascertain if the money which I had left there, stated in my will, had been claimed, and also liking the place, I returned to Melbourne, and took a lodging there over a stationer's shop. It happened one day, that my landlord and his wife had a quarrel, and high words ensued, they became so loud in their anger with each other, that I got up to shut my door, when the words 'Roydenhurst again! you're always on with me about that dreadful place,' caught my ear. You may imagine how this startled me. I listened, and distinctly heard my name 'Culverton' repeated by one of them. Was it a delusion on my part? could I have really heard this? To remain in suspense was impossible, so I rang the bell. It was some time before any notice was taken of it, at last the woman entered. I looked eagerly at her, but could not recognise in her face any one I had ever seen. I made her remain, while I rang for her husband, who came so briskly into the room, so blandly 'hoped I was well,' that I verily believe he thought I had invited him to tea, which happened to be on the table; it was extraordinary, the sudden change in his countenance, when I told him what I had heard them say; they both became so frightened—I suppose to find 'the heir,' as they called me, was alive, whom they and every one believed dead; that it was a considerable time before I could get anything out of them."

"But did you find out their names, and

where they came from ?" asked Sir Philip, as his companion paused in his narrative.

".Yes, and when I looked again at the woman, I thought that I had seen her before, but could not remember where, until she told me she had been formerly a servant at Roydenhurst; and the man, her husband, had been clerk to my father's agent years ago."

"Indeed!" Sir Philip exclaimed, "did they tell you how they made the discovery of the letter you speak of, and which, Culverton, has so happily brought you home?"

"Well, with some trouble I got it out of them. It appears these people had some law business on hand, and the lawyer they employed, who was also a friend, happened to be mixed up with that scoundrel Fortiswood's affairs, and discovered the whole thing. They lost their lawsuit or whatever the business was, and came over to Australia to seek their fortune." Again he paused and rested awhile, then he said, "Moreton, a man who for years has scarcely opened his lips, who has lived alone as I have done, finds talking somewhat difficult."

"Don't distress yourself, Culverton. I know enough of your story to guess the rest."

"No, I must go on and tell you all. Well, I was afraid these people were not telling me the truth, so I bribed them, to give me some proof of the veracity of their statement, and then they produced a letter, which they had received from their friend the lawyer, a Mr. Drummond, which alluded to Fortiswood being about to sell the Roydenhurst property, and he held 'the secret' which was to help him to some advantage. Now, I must get at this man Drummond, whose address they gave me, but he is out of town."

Sir Philip smiled when he had heard the end of the discovery, and was on the point of exclaiming "impostors," feeling quite sure they were the people who had so cleverly imposed on Mr. Penhorm; but he saw his companion could not bear the shadow of any doubt as to their statement being true. Moreover, he appeared too exhausted with talking to say any more about that circumstance. Sir Philip pressed him to let some wine be sent for, but he refused it, saying he should be all right presently; then he added, in a low tone—

"Moreton, I have not long to live, but to die at Roydenhurst has for years been my prayer, and now there may be months and even years of law, and anxiety to endure, before I may get it from the fellow who holds possession."

"No," replied Sir Philip, "there will be no great delay, nor any difficulty, for I know the 'fellow,' as you call him, Culverton, and I am sure you will get every acre of it back."

"Thank God," fervently exclaimed the invalid, adding, "but I don't deserve it, Moreton."

"Come, let us leave this dingy room,

Culverton; you will dine with me at my hotel to-day," said Sir Philip.

" No, not to-day, I must try to find out my sisters, and break to them the news of my existence, that is," he added, " if I find that letter of my father's. Can you help me to find them, if they are living ? "

" Yes," replied Sir Philip, " that I will my good fellow," and laying his hand kindly on his shoulder, he added, " you must first put yourself under medical treatment for that cough; you are not in a state to do anything at present, come, I shall not lose sight of you again; " nor did he, but after taking him to his hotel, he put him under Dr. Watson's care, who soon discovered that some anxiety was preying on his mind, which retarded his recovery, and he advised Sir Philip to tell him at once that he was himself the purchaser of his old estate. His astonishment, and the expressive joy this information threw him into, so excited him, that Dr. Watson ordered him to be kept perfectly quiet, and he recommended his friend not to see him for a day or so. In the meantime, Sir Philip determined to find out Mr. Drummond, and endeavour to procure the letter in question.

The following day, without sending in his card, or giving his name, he told a clerk, who was alone in the office, that he wished to see Mr. Drummond on private business, consequently he was shown into the back room, where that gentleman sat reading a newspaper. He immediately rose and looked enquiringly at the stranger.

" Mr. Drummond, I presume ! " said Sir Philip.

" The same, sir, at your service."

" I am come, sir, on behalf of Sir Richard Culverton, whose claim to the estates of Roydenhurst in the Co. of Cheshire can be easily proved."

" Indeed ! He thinks so, does he ? " said Mr. Drummond, " pray take a seat, sir, while we discuss this business."

" Thank you, I prefer standing."

"Well," continued Mr. Drummond, "and so your client expects to get back his mansion and lands? Ah, very desirable, sir, it is, that all old baronial manors be restored to their original possessors. The Culvertons of Roydenhurst, are, I believe, a very ancient family."

"They are, sir," replied Sir Philip impatiently.

"Well, but really, so your client expects to get all back cheap and easy, does he? Ah, that's good! I can tell him that the present owner of the property will dispute his claim. I expect, sir, we lawyers will have a deal of trouble with him; then looking knowingly at Sir Philip he added, "yes, we lawyers know our privileges, a little extra trouble and delay in our business are our perquisites, sir. Well, you were saying your client expected his estate back easy, ah!"

"Possibly," replied Sir Philip, "but have you not in your possession a letter written by the late Baronet to his son, Sir Richard Culverton?"

Mr. Drummond looked with astonishment at Sir Philip, measuring with his eye that tall man from head to foot, before he spoke.

" We really, sir, cannot answer questions of this sort, put in so extraordinary a manner and not in the usual way of business."

" It is," replied Sir Philip, " in the usual way of business, and I am here to request you will produce that letter," he said sternly.

" Ah, yes, that's likely," said Mr. Drummond coolly, " pray, sir, are you professionally employed (as I take it you are) by that individual, calling himself Sir Richard Culverton?"

"Yes," replied Sir Philip, " I am his brother-in-law, Sir Philip Moreton, and the purchaser of the Roydenhurst property ! "

Mr. Drummond started and coloured.

" Bless me ! I beg your pardon, I—I—really,. I indeed," he stammered out, " was not aware I had the honour to be addressing Sir Philip Moreton," and Mr. Drummond in his humility, bowed himself to a little distance, then somewhat recovering, he added, " the fact is, Sir Philip, we heard from a party in Melbourne only a week ago, that they had, singularly enough, seen Sir Richard Culverton, and they fully recognised him to be the heir to the estate. This intelligence necessarily makes us, you see, Sir Philip, very cautious in giving information to—to strangers."

" Probably it may, but I am here, sir, to request that you will deliver up to me the letter which the late Sir Godfrey Culverton left for his son."

Mr. Drummond hesitated, he did not like this prying into his secret—the secret which he had so long hugged, with the prospect of turning it to his advantage ; he could not bring himself to part with it all at once, and he was meditating on what terms he should propose to do so, when Sir Philip, seeing his hesitation, became impatient, and in a tone of severity, said—

" Sir, we know already from the people

who recognised Sir Richard Culverton the
contents of that letter; moreover, they informed Sir Richard that his signature was
wanting to effect a sale of the property,
therefore a forgery has been committed, sir."

Mr. Drummond turned deadly pale, and
was speechless, then suddenly conscious that
he was betraying himself, he stammered out
confusedly—

" I—I beg to assure you, Sir Philip, I
know nothing; the late Mr. Catchall was the
head of the firm when that business—I mean,
sir, Sir Philip, the sale of the property, and
indeed--"

" Sir," interposed Sir Philip, " that piece of
villainy I am not come here to discuss with
you, but to demand that letter addressed to
Sir Richard Culverton be delivered to me
immediately."

The discovery of the forgery frightened
Mr. Drummond, who began to think what
mischief an exposure might bring on the firm
" Drummond, late Catchall," therefore with-

out further delay, he proceeded doggedly to a shelf and took down a box, within which he took out another; unlocking it he drew forth the letter, and handed it silently to Sir Philip, who wishing to be certain it was the identical one he wanted, opened it, and glancing through it, said—

"Thank you, sir," then adding, "with regard to the trouble you contemplated, Mr. Drummond, from the present holder of Roydenhurst, I beg to inform you I shall with the greatest pleasure restore every acre of the property to the rightful owner, Sir Richard Culverton, without any law proceedings or trouble." Saying this, Sir Philip left the room and the office, leaving Mr. Drummond standing immovable and speechless. At last his rage burst forth. "Curse that dolt, that idiot Shuffles, with his blabbing tongue, he has spoilt my game; whoever heard of an estate got back in that way, no disputing the case, no trouble, no law, no costs, hang that old fool Shuffles," and here he continued to

swear at him, and in his rage knock down and
bang about everything in his way, that his
clerks in the office winked at each other, and
whispered—

"Something is up! Gov is in an awful wax."

After having had Dr. Watson's permission,
Sir Philip called to see the invalid; he found
him reclining on the sofa, looking ill and
apparently suffering.

" I am afraid you are not so well, Culverton,
are you in any pain ? " he asked.

"Rather," he replied, laying his hand on
his head, " the fact is, I can't sleep for anxiety
to find out the truth; if false, Moreton, about
my father, generous and noble as your intentions and wishes are, no power on earth
will make me accept your offer. I—I, shall
go back to die at—"

" There my good fellow," said Sir Philip,
interrupting him, and placing the letter in
his hand, " there my good fellow, that will
make you happier than you have been for
many a long day ; you have law on your side,

and can at this moment claim your estates, and now I shall leave you for a few days. when I come back, I shall hope to give you, Culverton, some tidings of your sisters."

Sir Richard Culverton became better in health from that day; he remained quietly at the hotel, there was no longer any fear of excitement doing him harm, his mind was at peace, he had at length obtained what his heart had been yearning after for years! When the friends again met, Sir Richard's first expressions were of his deep sense of gratitude to Sir Philip for all he had done for him; when Sir Philip stopped him, saying—

"Don't Culverton, talk to me, my dear fellow, of gratitude, for I owe you a debt of that sort which I can never repay."

Sir Richard looked surprised.

"Me! no, Moreton, not to me, I never did anything in my life for you; never showed you a good turn, I am sure."

"Yes, you have. Did you not forward a certain packet addresssed to my lawyer, to my charge, and did not that send me right and left to look for your sisters? Well, in that search, Culverton, I found a treasure, far brighter, purer, and more precious than all your nuggets; a wife, Richard!" and taking his hand warmly, " A brother! Your sister Laura is my wife!"

" Moreton!" laying his hand, now trembling with agitation, over Sir Philip's, "Moreton! You my brother! Is it true? Oh, how I thank God that I have lived to hear such happiness! All the torture, the pain, and misery I have endured for years is worth this joy! But, can it be possible—my little sister Laura your wife? Why, she was but a small child when I left home! And, oh, tell me of dear Jane; she and I were companions together."

We will not intrude on the family meeting—there is a sacredness in joy as well as sorrow—but we will now leave the happy party to talk over the past, and settle and plan for the future.

CHAPTER XXIV.

WE must now pass over five years of our story, and take our readers back to Roydenhurst, that lovely place, reminding us now in all its beauty of—

> "The stately homes of England, how beautiful they stand
> Amidst their tall, ancestral trees."

In a pretty, bright room, Jane Culverton is sitting, while two little boys are on the floor before her, with their toys and picture books.

" Look, Aunt Jane," exclaimed the eldest, a sturdy boy of four years old, "look, Aunt Jane, at this picture. Isn't it a monster ! "

" Let me see, Edward," said the other little fellow, a year younger, trying to snatch the book away.

" No, Richard, you tear it," and a rupture ensued, which ended in a cry.

" Children, I must send you to the nursery,"
and Miss Culverton rang the bell.

At this moment our old friend, Mrs. Tims,
entered.

" I thought, Miss Jane, I heard one of 'em
cry."

" Yes, Tims ; they have been very good
until now. I rang for their nurse."

" What is the matter, Master Richard?
Come to your old Tims. There, Miss Jane,
you mustn't think I am spoiling him ; but
the darling, he do so put me in mind of his
uncle, my own Master Richard ; he have his
pretty ways, and looks, when he was his age.
It does my old heart good to watch him, and
makes me feel — there, Miss Jane, you
knows what I means—'tis like living backwards."

And do we not all know what Mrs. Tims
means by " living backwards? " Has not the
sight of some object, some sensation, taken
us back in memory to the days of our youth?

The little boys having discovered the door

was open, had taken the opportunity to make their escape into the hall, which made Mrs. Tims hasten after them.

Sir Richard Culverton, though still an invalid, lived, and was happy, in the full enjoyment of his lovely place, showing by acts of love and charity to others the thankfulness and deep gratitude he felt for the mercies bestowed upon him.

Jane was devoted to her brother. To her tender care, her good nursing, and constant thoughtfulness for his comfort, he attributed his partial recovery. And this call for energy had benefited her own health, and enabled her to be the active superintendent of his affairs.

Sir Richard was known and beloved by all, and the drive to Roydenhurst became again a favourite one to neighbours far and near, who for many years had lost sight of the beautiful grounds.

Winter has passed, and summer in all its glory has arrived. Sunbeams are glistening through the trees, or playing hide-and-seek among the shrubs and flowers, defying even the shadows of the tall stately trees to spoil their sport.

A happy party are sailing on the lake in that graceful yacht. In former days sailing used to be Jane Culverton's and her brother's great delight—and it is so again, under the guidance of the old faithful sailor, Jack's son-in-law.

The yacht is gliding gently round an island, while from the drawing-room window, prettier and more charming than ever, in that little cap—scarcely to be called a cap—but which she considers to be matronly, Laura stands, watching the happy party, with Sir Philip by her side; he ready booted and spurred for a ride, and waiting for his horse.

"I am very glad to see Perkins is bringing up that boy of his so well," said Laura, pointing to a boy who just then appeared on the lawn with a wheelbarrow.

"Yes; Baxter says he will make a capital

gardener. I was thinking of having him at Kemberton, but perhaps on account of his father's antecedents there, it will be better for the boy to remain here."

" Yes, I think so too; he might hear things said of his father. But Richard appears to have great confidence in Perkins, and to have lately placed him in a higher post. I hope he really deserves it," said Laura.

" I believe he does, my dear. It was only yesterday that he was expressing to me his deep sense of unworthiness to be in such a position of trust. Perkins is very grateful, and for every mark of favour I show him expresses himself so well, testifying that he does not forget the past; nor indeed, can he. No forgiveness can ever blot out from memory a crime once committed."

" No, indeed," replied Laura, " or there would be no remorse, no real repentance; and without that, there can be no genuine gratitude. I always admire Milton's Eve when hailed by Adam, 'Eve rightly called the Mother of Mankind,' she expresses her sense of unworthiness so beautifully.

> " To whom thus Eve with sad demeanour meek :
> Ill worthy I, such title should belong
> To me, transgressor; who, for thee ordained
> A help, became thy snare ; to me reproach
> Rather belongs, distrust, and all dispraise ;
> But infinite in pardon was my Judge,
> That I, who first brought death on all, am graced
> The source of Life."

" Yes, that is very beautiful," said Sir Philip. " You must teach me, Laura, to know more of Milton's ' Eve.' "

" Well, there is one thing she did, which I shall certainly not teach you, and that is, she was the first to suggest, and the first to carry out, a separation from her husband. Now, that was very naughty of her."

Sir Philip laughed, and replied—

" You think, Laura, dear, she instituted the Divorce Court, do you ! But who taught you to be so Miltonic ? "

" Mr. Courtley ; I may thank him for all I

know of the great poet. He was continually quoting passages from one or other of his poems; but," she added, looking playfully in her husband's face, " I don't think, Philip, you half liked Mr. Courtley. You were rather puzzled at his continued compliments to the ladies."

" Was I ! How did I show it ? "

" Oh, by sitting bolt upright in your chair, and looking grave, and never saying a word."

" But taking notice of everything," he said. " Well I have grown wiser since those days, and, Laura, I have made a grand discovery."

" Have you ! What is it ? " she asked.

" That nothing takes selfishness, singularity, sooner out of man—in short, improves him more—than matrimony, and I mean to recommend it to all my friends ! But look, here is my horse," he added, as the groom passed with it to the door. " What a fine creature that animal is ! "

"Yes," said Laura, gaily, "just like his dear master—noble, good and handsome."

When Sir Philip reached the door, he turned to look at Laura, and said—

"Take care of yourself, love, and when I come back we must talk about taking leave of Roydenhurst."

THE END.

Printed by REMINGTON & Co., 5, Arundel Street, Strand, W.C.

www.ingramcontent.com/pod-product-compliance
Lightning Source LLC
Chambersburg PA
CBHW020850020726
47497CB00005B/1336